Bloody Seven

A Renegade Novella

K.M. Baker

Copyright © 2025 by K.M. Baker

All rights reserved.

No part of this publication may be reproduced, stored in a retrieval system, or transmitted in any from or by any means, without written permission from the publisher, except as permitted by U.S. copyright law. For permissions contact: kmbakerauthor@gmail.com

This novel is entirely a work of fiction. The names, characters, and incidents portrayed in it are the work of the authors imagination. Any resemblance to actual persons, living or dead, events or localities is entirely coincidental. All songs, song tiles and lyrics contained in this book are the property of the respective songwriters and copyright holders. Designations used by companies to distinguish their products are often claimed as trademarks. All brand makes and product names used in this book and on its cover are trade names, service marks, trademarks, and registered trademarks of their respective owners.

Cover design: Maree Rose

Editor: Taylor at Deliciously Dark Editing

Content Warning

Poppy and Corbin's story is a prequel novella that ends on a cliffhanger.

Please be aware this is a dark romance. This book contains explicit 18+ content that I do not condone outside of a fictional world. As always please review the below content warnings and proceed with caution.

If you have any questions or feel like anything should be added to this list, please do not hesitate to reach out to me via email at KMBakerauthor@gmail.com

Content warnings:

Adult language, Alcohol use, Blood, Death, Loss of a Loved One (on page - Not a MC), Mention of parent death, Mentions of Suicide, Mentions of Suicidal Ideation, Murder, Religion inspired violence, Stabbing, Torture, Trauma, Violence

To anyone looking for a dose of feminine rage,
revenge, and man who loves being called a good boy.

Playlist

Prologue - Levitate – Sleep Token

Chapter 1 - Peggy - Villains Aren't Born (They're Made)

Chapter 2 - Welcome To New York - Taylor Swift (Taylor's Version)

Chapter 3 - First Date – blink-182

Chapter 4 - Electric Love - BORNS

Chapter 5 - bloody valentine - MGK

Chapter 6 – Nightmare – Halsey

Chapter 7 - No More Tomorrow - Feverhill

Chapter 8 - better off without me – Matt Hansen

Chapter 9 - new way out – Poppy

Chapter 10 - Give You Love - Alex Warren

Chapter 11 - Giving Back the Pain - Afterlife

Epilogue - Revolution – The Score

Prologue
Poppy - Six years ago

What if I give him a blowjob and let him finish in my mouth for once? The thought floods my mind as I try to figure out the perfect way to thank the man sitting across the table.

Fiancée. Light catches the oval diamond set on the perfectly sized white band on my left hand, and I can't help the smile that creeps across my face. While it was something I wished would happen, I never expected it to be today. Look at us, a Valentine's Day love story.

Drew catches the glint in my eyes, and he knows, without a word, that it's time to get out of here. The sooner we get back to the hotel, the better for both of us. Not that dinner was bad. I just have my thoughts set on how to reward my new fiancé and the fact that I get to call him that now.

He pulled the classic "put the ring in the dessert" before getting down on one knee and asking me to spend forever with him. Obviously, I said yes before promptly scarfing down the most delicious tiramisu. Can't let it go to waste.

My eyes land on Drew again as he flags down the server to get our bill while nudging his foot against mine under the table. "Are you ready to get out of here?"

"I think you know I am." I smirk devilishly.

"You're happy then?" His brows raise, and I shake my head at the ridiculous question.

"I can show you exactly how happy I am at the hotel," I tease, making him laugh under his breath.

He finishes paying the server, who gives us another congratulations before helping me slip into my jacket and taking my hand. After making it outside, he leads me down the snow-covered sidewalk rather than stopping to hail a cab. It's cold, but we can still enjoy the short walk through the streets of New York City.

"Tonight's been perfect. I don't want it to end," he says with a faint hint of sadness, stopping me in my tracks.

While glancing up at him, I smile and say, "You and me, love."

A hand reaches up to cup my cheek as he leans down, pressing his lips to mine. This is exactly what I want. As I push up on my tiptoes to deepen the kiss, surprise fills me when he pulls back and shakes a finger in my face.

"Poppy, if I kiss you like that right now, they may get more of a show than they deserve." He points to some of the other couples walking across the street toward the subway.

I giggle and grab his hand, interlocking his fingers with mine again. "Guess we better get to that hotel. I have a busy night planned with my fiancé."

As we stroll forward, thoughts of our future wedding fill my mind. Maybe we can find a small barn with horses and a lake. I can picture him standing at our makeshift altar, waiting for me to walk down the aisle with a smile. I'm quickly brought back to reality when I remember it will just be the two of us.

A pang of sadness over my lack of family suddenly fills me, and I make the mental decision to talk to Drew about going to the courthouse for the wedding. Since he doesn't have family either, it may be the best option for us. We could probably even go next week. Sure, we just got engaged, but why wait?

With my thoughts on our impending nuptials, I don't have time to react to the strange man lunging at us with a knife as we walk past a dark alley. He knocks Drew down with one swing and drags him into the shadows, leaving me startled and alone on the sidewalk.

When I finally step into the alley to find them, the stranger is on top of the love of my life, holding a knife above his chest.

"Stop!" I cry out as the man stutters through a string of sentences that don't make much sense.

He starts calling Drew a sinner, saying how this will cleanse him and how he was chosen for this favor. The stranger plunges the knife into Drew's chest while calling out 'gluttony,' and I let out a gut-wrenching scream.

Shock has me immobile. I shake my head, blinking my eyes rapidly before eventually gathering enough brain power to try and shove the mystery assailant off of Drew.

You know how to protect yourself. Get your shit together.

It's all for nothing, though, because I'm too weak for it to make any sort of difference. The stranger shoves me with minimal effort, forcing me backward. My butt hits the snow-covered pavement before my back does, and then my head, knocking the wind out of me.

"WAIT YOUR TURN!" he yells before telling Drew he'll be able to enter the gates of Heaven soon with God's widespread arms welcoming him.

Tears begin to flood my eyes as the man rapidly plunges the knife in and out of Drew's chest six more times while rattling off each of the remaining seven deadly sins.

No, this isn't happening! I scramble to my feet. *No. No. No. I have to stop him. I can't live without Drew. I can still save him.* When I step forward again, the bloodied man turns his attention to me.

He moves slowly in my direction and away from Drew's limp body. I scream at the top of my lungs while scrambling backward. Luckily, I manage to make enough of a scene for people to finally notice there's a man holding a fucking knife, covered in blood, and chasing a helpless woman.

A bald man comes to my rescue, knocking the knife out of my assailant's hand with ease before propping him up in a seated position against a storefront. The attacker rocks back and forth, hugging his knees and muttering some kind of prayer in a hushed breath.

I run to Drew, hoping that by some miracle, he will pull through, even though there is blood everywhere. When I fall to the ground next to him and press my arms against his chest, I don't feel a heartbeat.

"DREW!" I yell as I shake his body, but he doesn't move.

Tears flood my vision, blurring my eyes and a woman steps next to me, placing her hand on my shoulder. I have no idea who she is, but it sounds like she's on the phone with someone. Everything around me is muffled as my sole focus remains on my fiancé.

"Please don't leave me," I sob, refusing to believe that our perfect night is ending with my worst possible nightmare. "Please," I say with a shaky breath.

He isn't moving, and I can't find a pulse. There's so much blood, and it's on me now too. Finally, after a harsh realization, my brain reconciles the fact that Drew is dead. He isn't going to ever wake up again.

My eyes swirl around the crimson scene before me. Today was supposed to represent love, not loss. Pain and sorrow begin to consume every cell of my body. It feels like someone's reaching inside my chest and ripping my heart from it.

I breathe heavily as I slowly stand, covered in my now dead fiancé's blood, and walk out to the street with shaky hands. *I can't bring him back. He's gone. That fucking psycho stole our future.*

"YOU!" I seethe while trembling violently as the assailant comes into view.

The sick fucker lets out a manic laugh while continuing to mutter bible verses. The bald man watching over him looks down briefly before focusing his attention back on whoever is on the other side of his phone call.

My lip curls up in disgust as my body rapidly cycles through all the stages of grief. Anger. I land on anger again and take a step forward, ready to show this asshole exactly how badly he fucked up. I may be weak, but he stole someone I love from me. He deserves to be punished before the cops haul him away and he ends up with a brief stay in a psych ward before getting released on a technicality. No, he needs to pay.

A sly smile crosses his face like he knows exactly what I'm thinking as he lifts his arms into the air while looking up at the sky.

"God will welcome me in his holy embrace," he says before reaching into his pocket to pull out another knife.

"No!" I scream and lunge in his direction, but it's too late.

The assailant slides the knife across his neck, leaving me to watch in horror as blood pools down the front of his chest. He makes a gurgling sound before his head droops forward and the bald man leans down to check his pulse.

"He's dead," the bald man says, and I'm unsure if he's talking to me or someone else, but my entire body slips into a state of shock.

Drew will never get the vengeance he deserves.

I'm forced to sit here, waiting for the police, while my mind replays his death over and over again. Life is taken as easily as it's given, and I'll never forget that again.

Chapter 1
Poppy - Present Day

I wonder whose blood will coat my hands this year. That's the first thought to cross my mind as my eyes blink open and I prepare to start my morning routine. Should that be concerning? Maybe, but I'm past the point of giving a fuck. I'll be out of this city before I know it and back to my day-to-day life in boring 'ol small-town Pennsylvania soon anyway.

After throwing off the covers and immediately gravitating to the coffee machine, I make my way to the hotel's balcony with my cup in hand. With a gentle push, the door slides open, letting me slip through before I take residence in the rickety chair in the corner.

Light inches its way across the landscape, brightening the city inch by inch, as the sun begins to break the darkness of the night. It's my own little playground full of people who are none the wiser because even in the light, darkness can find you. A sinister grin crosses my face as I take my first sip of the bitter liquid in my cup.

Chills run through my body as the caffeine hits my system, and I tuck a piece of my long, black, wavy hair behind my ear with a smile. There really is nothing better than that first sip of coffee in the morning. It's the only way to determine how the day will go.

Good coffee equals a good day.

Shitty coffee, well, I think that's self-explanatory.

I take a deep breath, letting the cool air fill my lungs. It's loud here, even at seven am, in the city that never sleeps. Shades of yellow and orange brighten the horizon between the buildings, and I watch in awe as a new day begins. No matter how much darkness there is throughout the rest of my life, watching the sunrise is one of my favorite things to do.

It's a fresh start, and tomorrow, I'll be purging the rage that's been building within me for the last year.

Every Valentine's Day, I come here for vengeance on the city that gave me my entire world, only to take it away just a few years later.

Drew and I met at a club in Manhattan on Valentine's Day eight years ago. I just turned twenty-one and had never been to a bar before. Shocking, I know, but I was the typical good girl who always followed the rules while everyone else partied it up behind their parents' backs.

My bestie, at the time, had a Valentine's Day trip planned with her boyfriend in the city and told me I had to tag along. She refused to let me stay home, even though I tried to insist there was no way I was crashing their weekend. It was a useless battle that she won.

The club we ended up at the next day was busy enough for her to feel confident I would find someone to spend my evening with. She's lucky that's how the night ended because she left me for the dance floor with her boyfriend a solid ten minutes after we arrived. I silently watched the two of them dancing while I sat awkwardly at some random table, feeling insecure.

When I looked around the club, everyone seemed so confident in themselves. They weren't stuck in their heads, like I was. The outfit Lilly encouraged me to wear made me even more uncomfortable, but she insisted I couldn't go out wearing the same things I wore at home. This was New York City, and a little black dress was required.

The whole idea of even being there intimidated me because I doubt any of these people grew up with the same restrictions I did.

I was eight when my mother was murdered, and it completely changed my father's outlook on life. He never let me leave his sight and always made sure I was hyper-aware of my surroundings. He would quiz me on my situational awareness every day we spent together until the day he passed away just before my nineteenth birthday.

In my teen years, he was more intense. I was told to watch for strange men anytime I would leave the house. It was pretty much drilled into my brain that I could be assaulted or murdered at any point in time for no reason at all. I was even put in self-defense classes to learn how to shoot guns and wield knives. A skill that most would find useless, but I'm thankful for it now.

That situational awareness led me to a pair of eyes watching me from across the club, not long after my bestie abandoned me. When my brown eyes locked on his, a nervous blush swept through me. Thankfully, it was too dark for him to see it. A small grace.

He smiled, and the corner of my mouth lifted into a flirtatious grin as he made his way across the room to my table. I almost took the cowardly way out and turned to run, but there was something about him that lured me in. It was like nothing else mattered. My father's warning still echoed in my mind, and I think it would make him proud to know I was at least thinking about being cautious.

The handsome stranger introduced himself as Drew and went on to tell me about how he was here with his buddy. He pointed over to a guy in the corner of the club with his tongue down some girl's throat, and I giggled. Apparently, his buddy left him to fend for himself, similar to what Lilly did to me.

The two of us spent the entire night getting to know each other. In some twist of fate, he grew up less than an hour from me. The next town over, to be exact. We had just met, but in that instant, he became my everything.

Before we left the club, he tried to introduce me to his buddy, and the guy was a total douche. I can't remember his name, or what he looked like, to save my life, but he couldn't even be bothered to give me a proper hello. Instead, he looked at me, briefly waved, and went back to sucking the girl's face.

When I asked Drew more about him as he walked me to my cab, he told me they were roommates in college, and they graduated from NYU the semester before. This was their first time meeting up after graduation.

Now that I think about it, I guess they didn't bother to stay in touch because over the next two years, I never saw that guy again, and Drew never talked about him.

I feel the emotions begin to pull at my chest. It was our tradition to come to New York City for our anniversary and we had a whole itinerary. The day before would be spent walking around the city, soaking up the different cultures. On Valentine's Day, we would go to dinner, and then the day after, we would spend an entire 24 hours tangled up in one another in our hotel room. Three days of bliss with the man I love every year.

I didn't realize our second anniversary would be our last. That psycho in the alley took him from me, and now I've spent more days without him than I spent with him. That thought is almost too much to bear.

Some days, his death feels like a distant dream, and others, it feels like it was just yesterday. They say you don't know what you've got until it's gone, but I don't always think that's true. Sometimes, you know exactly what you've got, and that makes it so much worse when it's gone. So many people spend their lives taking advantage of the things they should cherish the most. I'll never take a single thing for granted again.

After I returned home to plan Drew's funeral, a deadly mixture of hate, loss, love, yearning, pain, and trauma brewed inside of me. We just bought our house, and we were planning our future, but none of that mattered anymore. Every time I closed my eyes, I saw flashbacks of his attack. *The knife. The blood.*

A tear slips down my cheek, and I wipe it away aggressively. I should have been able to defend myself that night. With the training my father gave me, I should have been able to fight back to protect Drew. My fucking emotions got the best of me, and I stood there like a deer in headlights, unable to use any kind of rational thought. It's too late for me and Drew, but I will finish my quest to honor his memory.

After his funeral, which was only me having him buried, I stayed at his grave for hours. My fingers were frozen, and I was nearing frostbite, before I finally had the courage to go home, knowing what I had to do. I made a vow at his gravesite. I promised I would return to the city every year on our anniversary until he got the vengeance he was owed.

Seven men, seven years, seven deadly sins.

I spent my time before the first kill building up my strength and working through my grief. Exactly one year later—Gluttony was taken out. It didn't take long to find him either.

I was walking down the street late at night and noticed some sorry piece of shit that had a woman pushed up against a building, and I took it upon myself to give him what he deserved. He was clearly drunk and refused to listen when the woman tried to push him away, so I pulled the Taser from my purse and zapped him with it. He was disoriented for a few seconds giving the woman time to scurry away, and I stood there wondering if I was really ready to kill someone.

Spoiler alert, I did. I pulled a knife from my pocket and stabbed him seven times, taking the man's life, just like my Drew was taken from me. I didn't know his name, but it felt so fucking good to end him, knowing that because of me, he would never hurt another woman again.

The bloody snow threatened to pull me into memories of Drew, but I kept them at bay as I reached into my purse for the single red rose and dropped it on the man's chest. When I walked away, my skin buzzed with adrenaline.

That was six years ago. While I admit it was pure luck, I never got caught, and the rest of my first five kills have gone swimmingly. I became more methodical, but Gluttony, Pride, Envy, Greed, and Sloth all died the same way. A Taser to the neck before being stabbed seven times and left with a red rose on their chest.

It took a few years, but after year four, the cops recognized my signature pattern, and I earned a name for myself. The Cupid Killer.

It's a silly name, but the authorities thought they were clever since my kills always take place on Valentine's Day, and a rose is left behind. They have no idea who they're looking for or why I'm killing people because the only thing to connect my victims is the fact that they're men, but with each kill, Drew's memory lives on through me.

Lust is this year's sin, and tomorrow, someone will be painted in blood. The same beautiful shade of crimson that this holiday is represented by. The color that still haunts my dreams every time I close my eyes. I take another sip of my coffee before sucking in a deep breath to center myself.

It's almost time to go back inside to get dressed. Today, I'll walk the streets of the city, scouting out my next victim. I was careless the first year, but I learned from it and found ways to prevent myself from getting caught. It's not foolproof, but this way ensures my kills are fueled by something more stable than emotions.

The last few vibrant colors from the sunrise fade, and the light of the day shines bright across the city. The new day has officially begun, and there isn't a cloud in sight. With a smile, I stand and walk back into my hotel room.

I drop the paper coffee cup in the trash and saunter to my suitcase to grab today's outfit. It's always the same: black leggings, a black sweater, and a black jacket. You'd think I like the color black or something.

I dress quickly, combing out my wavy hair before giving myself a quick glance in the mirror. I've grown so much over the last six years. I doubt Drew would even recognize the woman I am now, and that makes my heart hurt.

My hand reaches up to touch my cheek, the same pale skin that he used to touch. The look in my eyes is more vacant than ever. Any joy that once filled them was taken from me when he died.

Next year, I'll complete my promise, and I don't know exactly what that means for my future. I don't know if I'll be able to let go of this pain I've held onto for so long, but that's a problem for next year. For now, my only focus is on Lust.

Chapter 2
Poppy

Why the fuck are there so many people out and about this early? The streets are bustling as I stalk down the sidewalk. I'm a killer on a normal day, but when I'm hungry, my mood is significantly worse.

Most people don't bother to look at me when I bump into them, on my quest to find the bagel place I read about online. Locals know the more you keep to yourself, the better you are. The only people to shoot me side-eyed glances are obviously tourists.

Tourists are fairly easy to pick out because they don't have anywhere to be. This city is constantly moving, and tourists move slower. You'll find them stopping by a storefront or pulling out their phones to take pictures.

I used to be like them, finding the beauty in the unique architecture or feeling the fascination of the many different cultures that somehow blend together to live synonymously. I don't feel much of anything anymore, with the exception of disgust and rage. It's taught me how to blend in. So much so that even when I'm not in the city for my annual hunts, I'm thinking about how I can prepare for the next one.

I continue down the street and notice a woman calling out to a young girl. My eyes land on the child running toward me with the woman, who I believe is her mother, waving her arms and trying to chase after her. I step in front of the little girl's path just before she can run past me, making her falter.

"It's not safe to run away from your mommy," I say as she looks up with innocent eyes. With any luck, that innocence will never prematurely know the darkness of the world.

"Valerie, we talked about this!" the woman yells again before leaning down to pick her up.

"Mommy!" The little girl giggles when her mother squeezes her tightly.

"Thank you so much," she tells me, but I can't stop myself from shaking my head with annoyance.

"You should be more careful. There's tons of freaks in this city," I say as I walk away.

I don't have it in me to be kind to her, even if it was an accident. It only takes one wrong move, and some fucking creep has the opportunity he needs to swoop in long enough for her to never see her daughter again. It's just irresponsible.

This encounter reminds me of when I killed Pride.

The snow was heavy due to a superstorm that blew its way through the city. Even with the inclement weather, it didn't stop the tourists from showing up in full force. New York City on Valentine's Day is just too tempting, I suppose.

As I walked down the street an altercation between a man in a fancy suit and a mother with a small child caught my attention.

The man had his hair slicked back and was pointing a finger in the woman's face while screaming about how she should've had a better eye on her daughter.

The little girl wasn't paying attention and bumped into him, scuffing up his shoes. He made sure everyone around could hear about how his shoes probably cost more than she made in a month.

The woman apologized profusely while the man continued blabbing about how expensive his stupid fucking shoes were. As soon as she walked away, he carried on walking down the street, muttering to himself, with me following closely behind.

A woman with long brown curled hair, dressed like a model, walked by and he made sure he hit on her. He tried asking her out, and when she told him no, he said he would buy her whatever she wanted if she agreed to go on a date with him. She said no again and practically ran away. That was all I needed to choose him as the Pride kill.

I secretly followed him, until he took a phone call saying he would meet some girl next to Madison Square Park and made sure I met him there first.

When I did, I praised how he looked and gave him some story about how he would be my hero if he helped me save a kitten from a tree. Fucking idiot. How many kittens do you think are stuck in trees in New York City, in February?

It took a little convincing, but he couldn't pass up the opportunity to be applauded, so he followed me to where there was enough cover to keep us out of sight.

Once in place, I wasted no time, hitting him with the Taser and stabbing him over and over. All that pride did him no good because his blood stained the snow the same as anyone else's would. We all bleed red. I dropped my rose on his chest and strolled away like nothing happened.

Bringing myself back from my thoughts, I turn the corner, and the bagel shop finally comes into view. I push the door open and step to the counter, completely unsure of what I plan on ordering. Normally when I go to a new place, I study the menu, but my dumbass didn't this time.

My gaze lands on the guy behind the counter, and when my eyes meet his, there's a strange pang in my chest. The feeling startles me because the last time I felt something like this was the first time I saw Drew. When I look into this man's emerald eyes, I find myself getting lost in them. His mouth tilts up before he chuckles, making me scowl. What the hell is he laughing at?

"How can I help you, cupid?"

I narrow my eyes and cross my arms over my chest. "Cupid?"

"You looked a little lovestruck for a moment." He raises his brows with confidence. This smug bastard.

"I was not," I say way too defensively. I don't even believe myself.

"If you say so." He laughs again, and this time, I notice the dimples on both sides of his cheeks.

No, stop it, I tell myself and glare in his direction. "I was just trying to figure out what to order. Is this how you treat all of your customers? What would your owner think of that?"

"Only the pretty ones." He steps out of view to fiddle with something. "And I am the owner, so I would say he doesn't mind one bit."

My jaw practically drops to the floor. I would have never guessed he was the owner. "Fine. What do you recommend?"

"Just hang on a sec. I'll give you the best thing this place has to offer. You can thank me for it after."

"Should I be concerned? That sounded kind of forward."

"Get that mind out of the gutter, cupid."

"Stop calling me that," I say as he comes back into view with a sandwich in hand.

"No allergies, right?" he asks.

The question startles me for a moment. He might be the first person to show me even the tiniest bit of concern in years. I'm usually invisible to everyone.

I wish I was still friends with Lilly at times like this. We could gossip about the cute bagel boy, and how this whole conversation is embarrassingly awkward, but I pushed her away. My life isn't important. It's better that my personal things stay on the back burner until I'm able to fulfill my promise to Drew.

"No," I grit out.

"Try this, and if you don't like it, it's free. If you do like it, then you have to meet me at a party tonight because your money's no good here."

"And what if I don't want to meet you at a party tonight?" I counter, refusing to grab the sandwich from his hand just yet.

This could be the perfect opportunity to set up my kill for tomorrow. I could kill him in some dark parking lot after we leave whatever party he wants me to go to, and he proves to be a scumbag. Lust would be the sin to just willingly walk itself directly into my knife.

"It's an 'I hate Valentine's Day' party if that makes the decision any easier."

"I do hate Valentine's Day," I confess, letting a bit of vulnerability slip out without even thinking. Immediately, I put my walls in place and eye him again.

"Make a choice, cupid," he says while waving the sandwich in my face. "It smells good, doesn't it?"

I reach up and snatch it from his hand. "You don't have a New York accent," I point out as I inspect the strange food.

"Sure don't. I've only been in the city for a few years. I went to college here and decided to stay after graduation. I'm originally from eastern Ohio."

That takes me back a little. Ohio? I suppose this city is full of people from all over, but when you go into bagel shops that are as well-known as this one, they're usually family-owned and passed on from generation to generation. It takes balls to be an outsider trying to open a shop with something this city deems as sacred.

He watches me intently as I bring the sandwich to my mouth for a taste, and when a soft moan leaves me, his gaze flicks to my lips. My eyes widen with immediate regret and I chew as fast as possible.

"So, I take it you enjoyed that bite?" A nice smug tone meets my ears.

Fuck. I hate admitting someone else is right. "It was alright."

"Alright? That moan suggested otherwise."

"I did not moan." A lie, I know.

"You most definitely did, and if there wasn't a counter between us, I might be tempted to do something about it."

"Careful, I'm not like most girls. I will throat punch you before you even see it coming. You would be on the ground begging for me to go easy on you."

"Oh, so you're flirting with me now?" He smirks.

"If you get turned on by violence, then maybe." I shrug.

"It's less about the violence and more about the idea of a woman taking control. You might just be my soulmate."

His confession startles me. "I am not your soulmate."

"If you say so. Anyway, how did the sandwich do?"

"It was fine." I roll my eyes. "What was it?"

"My go-to order. A jalapeno cheddar bagel with pastrami, egg, cheddar cheese, scallion cream cheese, and brown mustard. In other words, an orgasm in your mouth."

"That was not–"

"You moaned." He raises a brow after cutting me off.

My eyes bounce between his. He's so direct. I've never met anyone as bold as him who also has a desire to be submissive. There's a challenge in his eyes, like he's willing me to take the lead, but I'm not here for any of that.

"What's your name?" I ask while taking another bite. It takes all of my willpower to keep myself from moaning again. The explosion of flavor is like nothing I've ever experienced before.

"Corbin." He reaches a hand over the counter, prompting me to shake it.

"Nice to meet you, Corbin. I'm Poppy."

"Well, shit. Now I feel like I missed an opportunity by not giving you a poppy seed bagel. I could have claimed it was fate or something that I gave you the same kind of bread you share a name with."

"I've heard it a thousand times. It never would have worked."

"Good to know." He grins, and those dimples appear again. "Give me an honest review. Did you like it?"

"Honestly? It was the best bagel sandwich I've ever had. Thank you." I take another bite, knowing his eyes are practically burning into my skin.

"You can thank me later at the party."

Crap. I forgot that was part of this little bargain he concocted. The stark reminder jolts me back to reality. I shouldn't be flirting with him. What the hell has gotten into me?

"You wouldn't leave a guy hanging, would you?"

"I absolutely would, but luckily for you, I don't have plans tonight."

"Great, where can I pick you up?"

"How about I meet you there?" I suggest, because I don't want him coming to my hotel.

"I suppose that will be fine, cupid. At least give me your number so I can check in to make sure you don't leave me high and dry."

"No, I don't think so. You'll just have to hope I'm an honorable woman." I finish off the sandwich, licking my fingers. "If you've got a pen and paper, you can write down the address for me."

"Pen and paper? How old school," he comments as he walks toward the register to pick up a pen. A few scribbles later, a paper is extended in my direction, and I grab it.

"I'll see you tonight. Is there a dress code?"

"Be there at eight, and wear whatever you feel comfortable in." His gaze darkens as his eyes trail down my body.

"Gotcha." I nod and point my finger awkwardly at him before turning to leave. "I'll see you then."

"It'll be the second-best part of my day," he remarks as I walk out the door.

He thinks meeting me somehow made his day better, but that couldn't be any further from the truth. Meeting me sealed his fate. He won't live past Valentine's Day.

Strangely, I find myself hesitating because he hasn't done anything that would warrant being my next victim. Can I kill an innocent person? Will that make me any better than the stranger who killed Drew?

With how flirty the guy is, it will only be a matter of time before he puts his hands on me without my permission. That's what I allow myself to believe in order to justify saying yes to meeting him at the party.

Doubt begins to consume me, though. Deep down, there's a part of me that only wants to kill him because he makes me feel something for the first time in years. That thought alone makes this so much more complicated.

Chapter 3
Corbin

By the time I walk into the bar, the party is in full swing. If I had to guess, some of these people likely came directly after work to start their nightly binge. Tito's has become one of the more popular spots in the neighborhood because of all the events they host.

Mondays are ladies' night, followed by a Tuesday gentleman's evening, a monthly speed dating event, karaoke, and really just any possible reason to bring people in to spend money. I glance around at the tacky decor, full of black hearts and red roses, trying to hold back a laugh. My buddy really outdid himself, but he knows how to run a business.

Trent's been trying to get me to come to his 'I hate Valentine's Day' party for years now, but I always tell him no. Unlike most places, he hosts his annual gathering the day before the holiday because, according to him, "It's the best way to find a date for Valentine's Day." A fool-proof method that he's had a one hundred percent success rate with.

I hate to admit it, but the fucker is clever. Most people who attend these kinds of parties are here under the false guise that they hate the entire concept of the day. In reality, they're just looking for someone to connect with, even if they say they aren't. Human connection is the one thing we all naturally crave.

After a few drinks, most of these people will find their way to the dance floor, and by the end of the night, they will pair off to head to their tiny-ass apartments and fuck like rabbits for maybe an hour before passing out.

This is the kind of party I would have been all over in my early twenties. I used to be exactly like all of them, especially if there was a chance for a meaningless hookup. I can't even begin to guess the number of women I've woken up to in the morning after a bar night with no idea who they are.

That's just not who I am anymore. Life and age have caught up to me, not that I'm old by any means. Thirty is still young enough to hit the party scene, but I've started to really wonder if things would be different with a partner by my side.

The sandwich shop has kept me busy enough that I don't usually think about how I've been alone for years now. I have to pour my time into something, though.

As I walk up to the bar, I'm met with a look of surprise on my buddy Trent's face. It's brief before it turns into a smug smile.

"Tired of staying home and jacking off when someone else can do it for you?"

"You're disgusting, you know that?" I roll my eyes.

"Wish I could say that was the first time I've been told that."

"Maybe you should take it under advisement then," I suggest, and he shakes his head.

"Boss!" one of the bartenders calls out, and he waves her off.

"You two can figure it out yourselves for a few minutes. That's why I pay you, isn't it? I'm having a conversation." He dismisses them.

"You should be nicer to your staff," I chuckle because Trent is and has always been a dick.

He nudges his head toward the packed bar. "Have you at least checked out the crowd? There are some bombshells here tonight."

I turn and look to appease him. The place is full of women in black and red outfits, some of them putting more effort into their looks than others. A few are wearing what looks to be lingerie while others took the more casual route.

One woman locks eyes with me, and I watch her deliberately eye fuck me. She gives me a half smile and waves the tips of her fingers, making me shake my head as I turn back to Trent. There's only one woman I'm interested in seeing tonight, and from the looks of it, she's not here yet.

I hope she doesn't stand me up. I'm not stupid. Asking her to come here made her uncomfortable, but even if she doesn't show up, at least Trent will get off my back about a night out.

"Give me a whiskey on the rocks, and don't worry about me," I say with a sharp undertone.

He eyes me wearily as he moves to the bottles on the wall behind him. He knows what I like, and there's nothing wrong with having a little liquid courage while I wait. I told her to be here at eight but figured I would come earlier to make sure there was no possible way I would miss her.

A glass is placed in front of me as Trent crosses his arms over his chest. "Okay, why are you really here?"

"I can't party?" I suggest making him roll his eyes.

"I've been trying to get you to come to my Valentine's Day party for years, and you've never shown up. In fact, you never come out at all anymore. The only reason you would be here on a night like this is because you're chasing some tail." He grins. "Please tell me Goody Boy Corbin is finally trying to get laid."

"It's not like that," I say, not denying the fact that I'm meeting someone tonight.

"I knew it! What does she look like? Is she hot? Does she have a sister? Do you want me to talk you up? I can tell her you save puppies or some shit like that."

"I want you to chill the fuck out and leave me be." I toss back the drink, knowing he's most likely going to fuck this up for me. I should have had her meet me somewhere else.

"Please tell me all about how he saved the puppies." A soft voice interrupts. "I think I would love that story."

I turn, and my heart skips a beat when my eyes land on the most beautiful woman I've ever seen. A strange sensation fills me, and I don't know what to think of it. All I know for certain is that I want to do whatever I can to make her mine.

I knew she was gorgeous at the sandwich shop in her leggings, but dressed like this? I have to actively control myself from getting a raging hard-on like a fucking teenager.

"You look stunning," I say as I bend down to kiss her on the cheek.

When I straighten myself back up, I notice her wide eyed as a shade of pink creeps onto her cheeks. She's wearing a black mini-dress that falls just above her knees with black boots. The sleeves of her dress fall loosely over her shoulders, and her hair is curled, making me want to run my fingers through it.

I wonder if she's the kind of girl who likes to have it pulled. The sound of her moaning after taking a bite of that sandwich earlier fills my thoughts again. Fuck, this girl could tell me to crawl around and bark like a dog, and I think I would.

"Hello? I believe I asked to hear about the puppies," she persists, keeping her eyes on Trent.

"I don't really think that's necessary," he concedes.

"And why is that?" she tosses back, eyeing him like she recognizes him from somewhere.

"Because you're clearly already smitten for my boy Corbin. He kissed your cheek, and you almost climaxed. You two should save yourselves some money and just go to Corbin's place to bang it out. The sex might be better when you're sober."

"This is the kind of company you like to keep?" she directs toward me.

"It's not my fault. We were roommates in college. I had to be friends with him."

"Yeah? What's the excuse for keeping him around now?" she jokes.

"Free booze." I laugh before turning toward Trent again. "Get the lady a drink. It's the least you can do after ruining my second first impression. I've got to do everything I can to salvage this date now."

"Uh, not a date," she insists.

"Wow, kind of harsh there, cupid. Hate to break it to you, but this is a date. I'll change your mind by the end of the night, and then the two of us will leave here with me escorting you to your place like a true gentleman."

"I'll take a Gin and tonic. And not that bottom shelf Gin that's going to give me gut rot either. Give me Hendrick's."

"Bossy little thing." Trent laughs before turning to make her drink.

"Oh, and I don't live in the city. My place is a hotel room."

As he hands the drink to her, he looks back over at me. "I like her. She's got a bit of fire. Might be worth keeping this one around."

"Thanks for the approval, Dad." I roll my eyes before giving Poppy my attention. "Let's go over there where he can't bother us."

"Aww, I was just warming up too." She smiles but lets me lead her across the bar to a small corner with tables that are roped off.

"V.I.P.?" she questions.

"It helps when you know the owner. Lots of perks."

"I take it Mr. Personality over there is the owner?"

"Indeed, he is. It's not too loud here, is it? I didn't think things through when I brought this party up. I just wanted an excuse to see you again, and it was the first thing that came to mind."

"It's fine. I can hear you loud and clear." She takes a sip of her drink, and her eyes roll back in her head.

"You have got to stop doing that," I confess before I can stop myself.

"Stop doing what?" she teases, like she knew exactly what she was doing.

"Okay, cupid. What's your story? Should I be concerned?"

She hesitates a bit but then tells me how she's only in town for a few days. I'm given vague details about her as she continuously shifts the conversation back to me.

She must have walls up, but I'm confident that with time, I'll can get her to open up more. Every barrier will come down, one at a time, because I'd be crazy if I didn't take a chance on a woman like her. Even if she isn't from the city, we could find a way to make things work.

Wait. Why am I so intrigued by someone that's basically a stranger? Is this what love at first sight feels like? No. I'm not in love, but I'm definitely infatuated.

The two of us spend the next hour or so talking and getting to know one another. I'm surprised by how easy it is to make conversation with her and how engaging it is. Any other time I've tried to date, I found myself tuning them out or picking out something about their mannerisms that bothered me. This one, though, she doesn't have a flaw in sight.

We polish off two more rounds of drinks before I gather enough courage to ask her to dance. Here we are, becoming one of the cliches of the night, and I can say with full confidence that I have zero regrets.

Chapter 4
Poppy

I came here with one thing in mind—murder—but the drinks and music have been a nice distraction. I'm starting to think I chose the wrong person to set my sights on because the guy standing in front of me hasn't given me any reason to kill him. He's actually one of the most attentive men I've met in almost a decade, which is beyond frustrating. I'm still entertaining spending time with him because I'm hoping he will prove to be someone deserving of death at some point.

We spent the first hour drinking and getting to know one another, which is not part of my usual pattern, but I can't seem to help myself. I'm blaming the Gin and those absolutely stunning dimples he flashes every time he smiles.

Disappointment settles in. I'm supposed to be here fulfilling my promise to Drew, but instead, I'm drooling over some guy. None of this is okay, and yet I can't stop myself.

It's crazy. I just met him. I'm supposed to kill him. Lust was supposed to be the easiest of the Seven Deadly Sins, but for some unknown fucking reason, this one has been the hardest so far.

Why do I want this guy near me, touching me? Why am I thinking about what he would be willing to do for me every time his tongue pops out to lick his lips after taking a drink? Would he beg me to let him fuck me? Would he let me call him my good little boy as I praise him? Clearly, I need to slow my drinking.

The longer I'm with him, the deeper my fantasies seem to grow. It's like there is an invisible cord pulling us together, that has me caught between a mixture of curiosity and anger. I can't explain.

If I let things progress beyond drinks, I could sully the memories of Drew, and if I don't at least try to explore this, I could go the entirety of my life without feeling this kind of connection again. Corbin's eyes bore into mine as though he can feel my inner turmoil. Why is the pull so strong?

He stands and extends a hand. "Dance with me?"

My eyes flick to the other side of the bar, where some women are grinding on men and others dancing with their friends.

I consider whether or not this is a good idea, but then those dimples appear again, and I can't help myself. It's just dancing, and even if things progress beyond that, maybe I can still kill him. He will probably end up being a 'one shot, stick it in for five seconds and then blow my load' kind of guy anyway. Now, that's something that deserves murder, not letting a woman finish first.

Corbin pulls me from my thoughts and onto the dance floor. He's quite a few inches taller than me, I'm guessing around 6'4, but that doesn't stop me from taking the lead. We find our spot amongst the others as the music bumps around us.

Electric Love by BORNS plays loudly, and I let the vibrations fill me as I lift one arm and throw it over his left shoulder. His hands land on my hips as he begins swaying me from side to side. The heat from his palms burns through my dress, making my heart slam in my chest.

Most men would pull me closer, limiting the space between us, but he keeps me at the respectable distance of my choice. Again, not ideal, considering I'm supposed to be finding a reason to kill him.

I move closer, feeling his hardened length brush against me as he takes a sharp breath. It's obvious he's affected by the contact, but he keeps himself focused intently on the way I move against him.

"Careful, cupid. I'm trying to be a gentleman. It's only the first date," he whispers in my ear.

I beam up at him, shaking my head. "Not a date."

His hands caress my body, and I get lost in the feel of his touch. One of them slides onto my neck, allowing his thumb to rub my jawline sensually, and I lose every bit of control I thought I had.

I tug him down and crash my lips to his, tasting the smoky whiskey residue on them. There may be a few regrets in the morning, but I don't care. I can't let this feeling pass by without giving it a chance.

We let the world fade away for a moment as his tongue slides along my bottom lip, sending shockwaves through me. The only thing I'm focused on is how much of a reprieve he is from the rage that has been consuming me.

I pull my lips back, my gaze full of nothing but pure lust as I say, "Take me home."

"I can't guarantee I'll be respectful if I do that, Poppy."

"I didn't ask you to be respectful," I admit as his eyes darken. "I asked you to take me home."

Nothing else needs to be said. He grabs my hand to lead us out of the bar and hails a cab. Within minutes, we're on our way to his place. This is so fucking irresponsible. I don't even know where he lives, and he could end up being some kind of crazed killer.

I let out a choked laugh, making him glance at me with concern.

"You okay?"

"Could be better," I tease as his hand rests on my thigh.

"How is that?" he asks like he doesn't already know.

"I think you know."

"I aim to please, cupid, but you'll have to use your words."

"Yeah? If you need me to give instructions, I think you'll find I have no issue with that."

"What do you want me to do, Poppy?"

"Kiss me, bagel boy," I breathe out, unsure why, but I want his lips on mine more than anything.

"Yes, ma'am," he replies as he leans forward to press his soft lips against mine.

I'm filled with the familiar feeling of lust as I part my lips and allow him to deepen the kiss. Electricity rushes through my body, igniting my limbs and taking my breath away. When he pulls back, I'm disappointed as I stare at him with wonder.

"We're almost there. Just a few minutes," he reassures me with a gentle squeeze on my thigh.

We spend the next few minutes in silence while the sounds from my thumping heart drown out the racing thoughts in my mind. What the fuck am I doing? Am I really going to sleep with him? The fact that I want to this badly makes me consider calling the whole thing off.

The cab finally stops, and Corbin opens the door. I waste no time placing my hand in his as he leads us up the stoop and buzzes us into his apartment building.

My usual self would be cataloging everything I see to make sure I have as much information as possible, but I'm blinded by whatever tension has built between us. I don't look around or care to see what number he presses on the elevator. When the elevator door closes, he's on me. His hands land on my hips, and he pushes me against the wall as his mouth lands on mine. I throw my arms over his shoulders, pulling him in before sliding my fingers through his brown hair. It's the perfect length to tug on.

He groans in my mouth, and it's enough for me to leave all of my previous doubts behind. That one sound shoots straight to my core, and I want to force him to make it again.

The elevator dings and we briefly separate as he leads me to his apartment. It's a short walk to the corner apartment, which makes me thankful. Maybe whoever lives next door won't hear us.

We step inside, and I expect to see the typical bachelor pad, but this place is the exact opposite. It's warm, inviting, and much bigger than I expected for a single man living in the city.

Directly in the entryway, there's a door to the right and a door to the left. As I kick my boots off to place them on a small shelf, he explains one is a closet, and the other is a bathroom. We step forward, and to our right is the kitchen with the main space directly in front of us. Between the kitchen and living room, there's a small hallway, which I would assume leads to a bedroom.

"Let me make you a drink. Gin and tonic, right?" he asks.

"Sure, but only if you have decent liquor," I tease.

I take it upon myself to walk around. There's a barn door on the opposite side of the living room. I slide it open, shocked to find it's a decent-sized bedroom. The deep brown color of the sheets matches the comforter and the decor on the walls. Inside is another door propped open, revealing the tiled floor of a second bathroom.

A two-bedroom apartment in New York City. This is the nail in the coffin I've been looking for, so I make my way out of the bedroom. There's no way a single man would have a home like this. There are even real plants in the corner of the living room by a small loveseat. Yeah, he's not single. As he walks toward me, I turn to face him and cross my arms over my chest.

"How long have you been married?"

His face contorts. "I'm not married."

"This is not the apartment of a single man who lives in New York City." I narrow my gaze.

"It is, actually. And I paid someone good money to make it look like this, thank you very much."

He paid someone to decorate? I guess that makes sense. Unfortunately, this means I still have no reason to kill him.

"Here, let's go sit. We don't have to do anything you don't want to."

"Are there drugs in this?" I blurt out before even thinking. Blame my father for the overactive thoughts.

"No, and I'll prove it to you." He grabs the drink and takes a big gulp before handing it back.

I eye him for a moment before deciding he isn't trying to roofie me and finally take a sip.

"You don't trust people, do you?" he asks.

"No," I admit before chugging the rest of the drink.

His eyes go wide as I stand, walk over to grab his whiskey, and down that one, too. I cross the apartment, placing the empty glasses on the kitchen counter before marching back to where he's seated and sliding onto his lap.

"No more games," I say, feeling his hard length pressing up against my center. His hands wrap around me, slipping under my dress to grab my ass.

"As you wish." He goes to lean in, but I put my palm on his chest, stopping him.

"This is only going to happen one way. I call the shots, and you do as you're told. If you have an issue with that, I'm afraid it will be better if I leave." I wait for him to tell me there's no way he's giving me control. Men never willingly give away control.

"Cupid, if you told me to lick the floor and beg for you, I would." He grins. "I don't know what it is about you, but I crave you. It sounds insane since we just met, but if doing what I'm told is what it takes to have you, it's a small price."

"Good boy," I say as I grab his shirt and pull his lips to mine. Licking the floor might be a bit extreme, but the idea of making him beg makes my body covet exactly that.

Chapter 5
Corbin

"Good boy," she says, making my stomach flip. This girl is going to be the death of me.

Her lips press against mine as my fingers grab her ass to pull her closer. Our tongues tangle with one another, and I find myself willingly holding back so she can take the lead like she wants.

She grinds against me, making me groan. "Cupid," I breathe out when her lips leave mine.

"You have no idea," she jokes, which is a bit confusing. "We shouldn't be doing this."

Oh, hell no. She's not about to call this off now. In the grand scheme of things, if she wanted to stop, I would, but she hasn't said no yet. There has to be some sort of battle going on in her head.

I lean in and press my lips to her neck while sliding my hands up her back. She moans and tilts her head to give me more access. "Tell me you want this," I say, wanting her to be in the moment with me.

"I do, but..." she trails off.

"If you want me to stop, that's all you have to say," reassuring her.

"I don't want you to stop," she admits. "I want you to go down on me."

Well, fuck. I pull back and look her in the eyes. There's a sparkle to them, almost like she's testing me somehow. She's daring me to tell her no.

Challenge accepted. I wrap an arm around her waist, holding her tightly while I use the other to help me stand from the loveseat. Her lips crash back onto mine as I maneuver us to my bedroom and flop her down on the edge of the bed.

Her heated gaze burns into me as I grin and fall to my knees in front of her. I grab one of her legs and pepper kisses up the inside of it, making her head tilt back. A soft whimper leaves her and goes straight to my cock, prompting me to repeat the process on the other side.

Her skin is so soft. I find myself consumed by it as I run my fingers up and down her legs before tossing one over each of my shoulders and wrapping my arms around her thighs to pull her closer to the edge. She dangles so far now that she falls back onto her elbows, giving me full access to what I want.

"You're not wearing panties," I point out with my heart pounding in my chest.

"Oops." She giggles.

This feels natural, like we've known each other for much longer than a few hours. There's an underlying level of comfort between us that has me at ease. "You've been like this all night, and I'm just now finding out?"

"Maybe."

"Cupid, you've got me enchanted."

"Make me feel good, Corbin," she whines.

I blow onto her center, watching in awe as her body shivers from the light contact of my breath. My head leans forward, and I trail my tongue lightly along her pussy, making her gasp.

"Be a good boy for me. Give me more."

Hearing her calling me a good boy makes my cock painfully hard. At this point, I'll give her whatever she wants if she keeps calling me that. I don't know who this woman is or what kind of seductive spell she's put me under, but here we are.

I dive in, my tongue lapping at her pussy, and it's everything I imagined it would be. I start off slowly, trying to get a feel for what she likes and take in every single soft sound she makes while I try a few different techniques.

Finally, I find a rhythm that she goes feral over, and her hips begin to grind along on my face while my tongue strokes her clit. Her fingers grip my hair, and she pulls me closer, smashing my face against her.

"Just like that. Don't stop!" she cries out as I keep up my pace.

Her moans make me want to spend the entire night on my knees, getting her off time and time again so I can hear them on repeat. It's like music to my ears, more so when it's my name.

Her fingers grip my hair tighter, making me wince, but I keep steady. After another moment, she jerks beneath me, forcing me to tighten my grip on her thighs to keep her in place as she chases her high.

"I'm coming!" she gasps as her hips buck up into my face again.

I look at her, in all her glory, as she finds her climax, and the hard demeanor she's been wearing for most of the night slips away, leaving a soft vulnerability that has me desperate for more.

Her fingers free themselves from my hair, and we lock eyes as her chest heaves up and down. She told me she wanted to take control, so I wait for her instruction, but the lengthy pause has me wondering if she might want to call off anything further and go back to her hotel to sleep.

Her eyes darken, and her voice fills with lust. "Do that again."

It takes me less than a second to have my mouth back on her pussy, licking and sucking my way to those sweet sounds. This time, I add two fingers to aid the process, and she takes everything I give her. Before long, she's riding out another climax, and it's fucking beautiful.

"I want you to fuck me, Corbin," she says.

I rise from my knees and pull her off the bed before grabbing the sides of her face and kissing her deeply. As I get lost in the soft feel of her lips, her hand slides down to rub my cock over my slacks, surprising me.

Reaching around, I find the zipper of her dress and slide it off her, watching the rise and fall of her chest before it pools on the floor. Finally, I take in the sight of her, and realize she wasn't wearing a bra either.

The soft curve of her hips gives way to a smaller waist and the perfectly-sized breasts. I sweep her wavy black hair over her shoulder before leaning down to kiss her collarbone. Goose bumps spread across her skin, but she reaches out to stop me.

"If I have to be naked, so do you."

She pulls my shirt over my head, tossing it across the room. Immediately, I know what her eyes land on, and it's not my tattoos. Several large scars cover my abdomen, prompting her to glide her hand over one of them.

"What happened?"

"It was a few years ago. It doesn't matter."

"Maybe it does." She studies the marks curiously.

"Poppy, do you really want to talk about my scars right now?"

"My rules, bagel boy. But I suppose you're right."

She unzips my pants before dragging them down with my boxer briefs in one swoop. My erect cock springs to attention, making her eyes widen. I mean, my dick is big, but it's not big enough to warrant someone having this kind of reaction.

"It won't hurt you." I laugh, and she slaps my shoulder.

"I know it won't hurt me, smartass. I've never seen a pierced one before."

A soft hand grabs my cock, making me jerk as she runs her thumb along the piercing on my tip. It takes everything inside me to keep myself from moving my hips forward and forcing her to jerk me.

Finally, her hand begins to move up and down. My eyes fall closed, and my head tilts back as I take in the pleasurable feeling.

"You like that, don't you?" she asks.

"I do."

"Do you want more?" Another question as she slowly pumps me at a torturous pace.

"Yes, please," I tell her, desiring everything she is willing to give.

"That's more like it. I love hearing you beg. Do it again. Beg me like a good boy."

"Please make me come, cupid."

"You're not very convincing. Tell me how needy you are for me. How desperately do you want to come?"

She's right. It's not convincing, but this isn't something I've had a ton of practice with. The more she tells me what to do though, the more I like it. My cock is painfully hard.

"Please, stroke me faster. I need to feel you."

"Is that so?" she teases. She strokes me a bit faster while tightening her grip.

"Fuck, if you keep up that pace, I might blow my load into your hand."

"We can't have any of that. You have to work a little harder." She giggles as she pulls her hand away.

I like the sound of her giggles, so I drop to my knees again and beg for her the way she deserves. "Please let me inside you, cupid."

She moves backward and slides herself onto the bed, never taking her eyes off of me. I stay on the floor like the good little boy she wants me to be, waiting for her to give me permission to join her. After what feels like forever, I hear her speak.

"Come here, Corbin," she commands.

I hesitate. "I'm not a dog," but still, I listen like one and move toward her.

"You listen perfectly. Look at you, doing so good. Do you want me?"

What kind of question is that? Of course I want her. "More than anything."

"Do you have a condom?"

"Yes, I do." I walk around the bed and tug the drawer on the nightstand, pulling out a condom and dangling it in the air in front of me.

"Put it on, bagel boy. Use me to make yourself come."

I don't need any more encouragement. I rip the foil package open and slide the condom over my dick, pinching the top to make room for my piercing and climb on top of her. My body hovers between her legs with my elbows on either side of her head for support.

Instead of immediately sliding into her like a normal man would, I lean in to kiss my way along her neck before moving lower to her chest and rolling her nipple between my teeth. She moans as her fingers tangle in my hair again.

I suck harder and feel her hips lift up into me, my cock lightly brushing against her wet center. The temptation is too much to resist. Slowly, I push inside her tight pussy while letting her get used to my size. My eyes fall closed for a brief moment before

I continue stimulating her body elsewhere to take her mind off of any potential discomfort.

When I'm fully seated, she exhales, and I use that moment to lock eyes with her. It's more sensual than it probably should be, but it feels right.

"More," she whispers, giving me permission.

This isn't like any other woman I've ever been with. I thrust into her, watching as her mouth pops open and those sweet sounds start escaping again.

"Harder," she says, prompting me to pick up my pace.

Her pussy spasms around me, making my dick twitch. I bring one of my hands down to her clit, rubbing light circles while my other hand keeps me propped up. Her moans get louder as I watch intently, making sure nothing I do causes her discomfort. Pleasure builds inside me, and I'm not sure how much longer I can last, but there's no way in hell I'm letting myself finish before she does.

"Don't stop!" she finally calls out. *Like I was going to*.

I thrust faster and harder, loving the way her pussy tightens against my cock as her fingers grip the bedspread next to her. "I know you want control, but please come for me again, cupid. I need to feel you give me everything."

That's the only encouragement she needs. Her entire body erupts as she clamps down on me, squeezing so tightly I lose my own control. I feel my body tense as I find myself on the precipice of my climax.

It takes a few more thrusts before I feel confident that her orgasm has started to recede, and I give into my pleasure. I grunt as satisfaction fills me while I continue to pump into her.

When I glance down, she appears exhausted but satisfied. The perfect combination. I flop onto the bed next to her, and she turns toward me, smiling. It's the perfect reason to press my lips to hers for a brief moment.

"The bathroom is there if you need it. I'll go grab us some water," I say, and she hums.

When I get to the kitchen, I pull the condom off and toss it in the trash, knowing I'll still have to wash up after she's done, but I want her to get in bed first.

I never thought I would think like this, but I'm getting cuddles tonight. She isn't going to leave me high and dry after having sex. I shake my head, concerned with my well-being, as I trudge back to the bedroom.

She's under the covers when I get there, so I place the glass on the nightstand and quickly find my way to the bathroom to rinse off before sliding into the bed next to her.

Her eyes pop open, and I lean in to press a peck on her nose, making her half-smile. "Get some rest. I'll order us breakfast in the morning."

"Lust is dangerous," she mutters before her eyes flutter closed.

I wrap my arm around her waist, pulling her closer to feel her warmth. I don't know who the hell this woman is, but I know I don't want her to leave my side.

Chapter 6
Poppy

I wake up realizing I fell asleep with Corbin. We had sex. Oh my god, what did I do? I'd like to blame it on having too much to drink, but that would be an outright lie.

Immediately, my mind starts to race. I lost sight of the goal and slept with someone while on a quest to get vengeance for my dead fiancé. I let lust pull me and willingly succumbed to it. I feel like a cliche, a disappointment.

Slowly, I move his hand off of my waist and carefully lower it before gently pulling back the covers. I need to think things through to decide what my plan is from here because today is Valentine's Day, and I'm supposed to fucking kill someone.

Part of me wants to kill Corbin for being so much of a temptation. He isn't a bad guy, even though he is the embodiment of lust in every way, shape, and form. I don't kill good people. No matter how my mind tries to justify things, Corbin will never be my Lust kill.

I need to get out of here and get my priorities straight. Letting these feelings for a man I barely know get in the way of what's really important isn't something I'm going to entertain any longer.

A throbbing pain radiates from the middle of my forehead, and I have to close my eyes to center myself. My body feels shaky, most likely from the massive amount of alcohol I drank last night. Great. To top everything off, I get to do all of this with a hangover.

Glancing around the room, I try to find my things. The little black dress lies in the corner, and when I pick it up, a brief flash of his mouth on my center fills my thoughts. He was so good at that.

Trying to be quiet when you're on the verge of a full-blown mental breakdown is easier said than done. I tiptoe across the room, pulling the zipper of the dress up as a sound comes from the bed.

I glance over to see Corbin has rolled over and is now lying on his back. My eyes study his face for a moment, taking in the sharpness of his jawline and the slight curve over the bridge of his nose. His hair is a tousled mess now, only adding to his overall attractiveness.

Guilt floods me as I tear my gaze from him, and sneak into his living room. The only other person I've felt this kind of instant attraction toward was Drew, and he was taken from me. Allowing myself to feel like this for someone else could leave them open to the same fate. Who's to say I wouldn't freeze up again in the face of danger?

My destiny is to fulfill this promise to Drew, and that's it. Fuck Valentine's Day and all the stupid things that come with it. A tear rolls down my cheek as I try to picture my life with

Drew, but all I can see is him bloodied in that alley. It hits me like a punch to the gut.

My knees give out, and I crumble to the floor, letting sorrow consume me as quietly as I possibly can. I shake my head and tuck the feelings inside because I have shit to do. I can't afford to let myself fall apart here. Getting out of this apartment before Corbin wakes up is best for everyone. Him being awake will only make leaving harder.

I stand and take a step toward the door, but I freeze when my eyes catch sight of a picture frame on his television stand. My face pales, and shivers course through me as I change direction and walk toward it.

A bright, smiling face stands out, pulling me to the photo like there's an invisible string connecting us. With a shaky hand, I reach down to grasp it. What stares back at me is a group of men with their arms around each other's shoulders and my very dead fiancé smiling like it's the best day of his life.

What the actual fuck?

My chest heaves as sorrow consumes me once again, but now it's mixed with anger. I'm not quiet and controlled with it this time. How is there a picture of Drew here? It looks like it was taken right around the time he and I met because he has the same haircut with the lines in it.

I glance at each of the faces in the picture and notice another that looks familiar. Is that Drew's douche friend from the club? I'm not positive because I didn't get that good of a look at him that night. He looks like someone else too, but I can't place it right now. I'm too angry. A total of six guys stand there, three of them familiar to me, and it makes me lose the last morsel of sanity I have left.

"WHAT IS THIS?!" I scream as I march back to the bedroom.

Corbin jolts awake just as I make it to the bed. His face is full of confusion as his wide eyes study me, trying to figure out what set me off. He looks at the photo that I shove toward his face, and he grimaces.

"Why do you have that? What's wrong with you?" he tosses out groggily.

"What the hell is this?" I ask again, demanding some sort of explanation that makes even the smallest bit of sense.

"Cupid, I'm going to need you to calm down," he says while running a hand up his face and back his hair.

"Stop calling me that!" I yell. "Why do you have a picture of my dead fiancé in your apartment?"

"Listen, it's the middle of the night, and I have no idea what you're going on about. That photo is of me and some of my brothers from college."

A fraternity? That doesn't make any sense. Drew never told me he was in a fraternity. "Drew wasn't in a fraternity," I state plainly, tossing the photo onto the bed and marching out of the room.

I stomp into the kitchen, pulling open drawers until I find what I'm looking for. My hand wraps around the base of the knife before I go back to where a very confused Corbin lies in bed.

"Poppy, you need to calm down," he tries, but I only see red.

Did he know who I was the entire time? Did he know Drew was my fiancé, and is that why he wanted to sleep with me? The dots finally connect. I think Corbin's friend from last night is the same douche that Drew tried to introduce me to the night he died. That's why he looked familiar.

Rage fills me, and I place the knife to Corbin's throat. "Tell me how you knew Drew for real, or I'll kill you."

He tries to push himself up, but I dig in deeper, holding my stance and not allowing him any space to sit up further without cutting himself.

"I mean it. You wouldn't be the first lying piece of shit I've held a knife to." I let it slip out. FUCK! I didn't mean to say that. My mind is in too many places right now.

"Poppy," Corbin states calmly. "Drew was one of my brothers in college. The six men in that picture were all inducted into The Collection at the same time. That's me, Drew, Trent, Devlin, Raiden, and Ghost. Well, his real name is Casper, but he goes by Ghost."

"No, Drew wasn't part of a fraternity. Why do you keep saying that? He would have told me."

"He didn't tell you because it's not the kind of brotherhood that people know about."

"You better talk faster because it's becoming more and more tempting to just slit your throat and just be done with it."

"Can you move that? I'll tell you what you want to know, but I'm not going to do it like this."

"You'll do it however I tell you to!" I assert and dig the knife into his skin, making blood drip down his neck.

It's not a deep cut, but it was enough to draw blood and make a point. I won't let him talk me down so he can get the upper hand and then call the cops on me or something. I'm sure I look like a crazy bitch, but that's how I feel, so whatever. I need to know how Drew is connected to this supposedly random man that just happened to be the first man I've had sex with in six years.

"Cupid, if you're thinking I knew you were Drew's girl, I swear to you I didn't. I knew he met someone, but I had no idea it was you."

"I said stop calling me that!" I sneer while digging the knife into his skin again. "Talk before I take away your ability to do it permanently."

"I already told you it's a brotherhood. Well, more of a society. They'll kill both of us if they find out you know anything, but I swear I'll explain."

His eyes are full of remorse. I can tell he is being sincere, so I pull back slightly to give him the chance to say whatever the fuck he's talking about. Maybe this means I can kill him after all.

"Then do it," I say, narrowing my eyes.

"We were inducted our freshman year of college. It's an elite group of men who take orders from those above them, and it's all extremely complicated. Essentially, we are assigned a woman to win over so we can pull their fortune into our control. We marry who they tell us to. It's a legacy that most of us are born into."

"That doesn't make any sense. I don't have any money or fortune, so why would Drew be with me if that were the case?"

"That's what you don't understand. He wasn't supposed to be with you. He went against The Collection. They had him killed."

No, I can't let myself believe that's true. I step away from Corbin and press my hands to my head, with the knife safely pointed away from my face. That would mean Drew died because of me. That makes this all so much worse than I originally thought.

"Lust was supposed to be easy!" I scream, letting the tears flood down my face.

"What are you talking about?" Corbin asks gently.

I'm tired of hearing him, feeling him, being near him. He messed all of this up. I wasn't supposed to catch feelings for the person I was meant to kill, and he most certainly wasn't supposed to be connected to Drew.

"I don't want to hear any more!" I yell, backing away and dropping the knife.

"Poppy!" he calls out, but I keep moving.

Just as I get to the door and lean down to grab my boots, his hand reaches out to grab my wrist. "Just talk to me," he pleads, and I notice he's still naked from last night.

"I don't want to!" I say, yanking my hand away. "Drew died because of me. I made him a promise, and I fully intend to follow through with it. Whatever stupid society you're talking about makes no difference. He's dead, and it's my job to get vengeance."

"That doesn't make any sense."

"It doesn't have to make sense to YOU," I sneer, opening the door. My head turns to give him one last glance. "Thank you for helping me remember what my priorities are. Do not follow me or try to find me." With that, I walk out of the door, stumbling as I pull my boots on.

"Poppy, stop!" he tries, but I don't care to hear what he has to say. It doesn't matter, and he can't exactly follow me while he's naked.

I rush out of the building with a fury building inside me. Is that how he was able to get such a nice apartment in the city? Surely owning a fucking sandwich shop isn't going to bring in the amount of money it would take to pay rent at this kind of place.

All of the red flags begin to fall into place as I step out to the street. It's nearly sunrise, and I have no clue where I am, but I pull out my phone and find I'm not that far from my hotel.

Without another thought, I hail a cab, give them the address, and get the fuck out of here before Corbin has a chance to try and come after me. I need my morning ritual of reflection before I can piece together what my next steps are going to be because this shit just got a hell of a lot more complicated.

Chapter 7
Poppy

The hotel comes into view, and I find myself starting to relax even though my mind is still racing. I politely thank the driver before striding up to my room. The first thing I do is strip myself of my clothing and head directly to the shower.

I can't believe I was weak enough to let another man touch me. I actually thought it was a good idea too, which makes it so much fucking worse. The water heats up, burning my skin as my mind tries to reconcile what I've learned this morning.

Drew was part of a secret society whose mission is to marry women in order to gain their fortunes. It doesn't seem like him at all. We were together for two years. He would have told me if he were part of some secret society. If he kept that from me, what else was he hiding?

I close my eyes, letting the water pour down my face. It feels like a warm embrace, and I find myself thinking about Corbin. How did someone of no consequence find a way to invade my thoughts so much in such a short amount of time?

I grab the small container of body wash and pour it onto my washcloth, scrubbing every bit of his scent off of me. He is nothing more than a one-night mistake. It will never happen again, and I will never see him again.

As soon as my shower is over, I dress and make myself a cup of coffee before heading to the balcony to watch the sunrise, just like I did yesterday. The colors aren't as prominent today, and I find myself thinking about how that aligns with my outlook beginning to fade. Yesterday seemed so bright but today feels dull. I watch as the sun crests over the horizon, officially beginning the day. Valentine's Day.

The last of my coffee is cold as I drink it down and take one last glance at the city's landscape before stepping inside. I have a few errands to run before I can come back here and wait until dark to complete my kill.

After changing into a casual pair of leggings, a black sweater, and a long black jacket, I head to the door to put my boots on. The next thing I know, I'm walking down the streets of Manhattan, similar to yesterday.

I opt to go in the opposite direction of my hotel today to avoid any chance of running into Corbin. As big as this city is, fate has a tendency to have a sick sense of humor, and I'm not willing to test it.

My first stop is with a small florist before I attempt to find another bagel shop. I slip inside to grab a small bundle of red roses and bring them to my nose, taking delight in the sweet smell.

"Those are beautiful," a woman says, interrupting my moment.

"They are."

"My best seller today. I hope whoever you plan to give them to loves them. I never get flowers." She smiles and steps away to the counter to ring someone up.

Ah yes, the gentle reminder that today is Valentine's Day. The day of love. I also hope whoever receives my rose tonight will love it, considering they will be dead. I put the bundle down, grab one single rose, and proceed to the counter to pay before hurrying out of the shop as I think of my Envy kill.

There were people arguing in the parking garage, and I couldn't help but listen.

"The only reason you even got that job was because of me," he slurred. "The boss wants to fuck you. You don't deserve to be the manager."

"I earned my position. Just because you helped me get hired doesn't mean I owe you anything."

"You owe me the same thing you gave the boss to get hired. A slut like you is always willing to suck a cock to get ahead. Why not mine?"

"You're drunk! Get away from me."

"You'll fuck everyone else but not me? I deserve it more than they do. You should thank me properly for everything you have. If it weren't for me, you would be homeless," he tossed out, prompting a knee to the balls that allowed her to run from his grasp.

It was good thinking on the woman's behalf because she was able to get away, and he became my target for the night. I was already behind on my choice, unsure of whether or not I would find one, and he stumbled along. Fate.

I slipped my gloves on, pulled the strings on the hoodie tighter to cover my face as much as possible, and yelled out, "Help!" from behind one of the cars in a dark corner. Again, it was fate that one of the lights just happened to be burnt out.

He came over curiously, and when he did, I hit him with the Taser before immediately plunging the knife in and out of his gut. He started to say something that I didn't want to hear, so the next stab landed in his throat.

Gurgles bubbled out of him while I continued the remaining stabs until I counted to seven. I stepped back and watched as the life drained out of him a bit slower than the rest before tossing my signature rose.

I shake my head and focus on today. The streets are already busy with people, which annoys me. The sooner I can get out of this city, the better. A bagel shop comes into view, and I decide this one is as good as any other, so I pop in and grab a plain bagel with cream cheese. If I were looking for the best option, I would have gone back to Corbin's. That's definitely not happening.

I spend most of the day wandering around the city, popping in and out of shops along the way and watching as many people as I can, before ending up in Times Square. I spot several couples walking by holding hands, and it makes me jealous.

Drew and I came to Times Square for our first anniversary and walked around, taking in everything like true tourists. It was the first time I had been to this part of the city, and everything felt so big. There were so many people and businesses. It was like another world. I guess compared to where I'm from, it is another world.

Drew had the purest soul. He never acted like he was from here and I hesitate with that thought. What if it's because he really wasn't from here? No. It doesn't matter. None of that matters, and I won't entertain these thoughts because he's dead. I won't disgrace his memory like that. Stupid Corbin making me have doubts.

Time flies by, and as it gets closer to sunset, I know it's time for me to go back to the hotel to change my clothes and grab what I need to make my kill. Lust will be dying tonight. I just have to find them first.

I make quick work, walking back to my hotel room and changing into my murder outfit. To be fair, it doesn't differ much from my regular outfit. It's just a pair of black slacks, a black long-sleeved shirt, and a black hoodie. Some years I add a black jacket. I always take it back to Pennsylvania and burn it after my kills.

Blending into the dark will be much easier this year because there's no snow. It's been warmer than it usually is in February due to a freak heatwave, but I don't mind.

I wrap my hair into a tight bun before securing an extra hair tie around it to keep it from falling out and then pull a beanie over my head for extra measure. Can't have one of my hairs accidently making it onto the crime scene, not that they would believe a woman like me would be capable of this level of brutal murder.

I grab my large cross-body purse and shove my knife into it, along with the long-stemmed rose, my Taser, and rubber gloves, as I prepare to find myself a victim worthy of death.

With that, I take the hoodie in one hand and head to the elevator. I'm more on edge than usual with anxiety creeping up when I push my way out of the front of the hotel. Once outside, I pull the hoodie over my head and walk toward the subway, making sure to hop on the Q to head into Brooklyn.

The train arrives right on time, and I slip into a seat, avoiding eye contact with anyone. The more invisible I am, the better. The ride is uneventful, for once, as we make stop after stop through lower Manhattan before crossing over the river.

I don't even know how many stops go by before I decide to get off, not knowing where I ended up. Somewhere in Brooklyn. It's all I need to know as I make my way off the train and up to the streets.

After glancing around to get my bearings, I start walking, unsure of where I'm heading, but I know I'll find what I'm looking for. This would have been so much easier if I could have just killed Corbin and been done with it. I'm letting this kill be controlled by emotion, which is exactly what I try to avoid.

I pass by a pizza shop, unable to resist the urge to dip in and grab a slice before I go on my way again. No sense in doing this on an empty stomach. There's a bar up ahead with music filling the streets, so I go in that direction. There has to be some lustful man around a bar, right?

As if the universe knew exactly what I was asking for, some guy walks toward me. Even in baggy slacks with a hoodie over my head, he still finds a way to objectify me.

"Hey gorgeous," the guy says as I walk past, and I already know where this is going to go. I may have just found Lust after all. These men really make it so easy by being nasty trash-bag human beings.

"No," I say, giving him a chance to walk away. He obviously doesn't.

"Oh, come on. Don't be like that. It's Valentine's Day. What's a beautiful girl like you doing all alone?"

I turn to face him with a flat expression. "Does it look like I want to be bothered by you?"

"It looks like you stopped to talk to me," he says, reaching out to place his hand on my waist.

I try to keep myself from recoiling because I don't want his hand on me, but it makes me feel better knowing I will kill him before the night is over. He had the opportunity to prove he wasn't a pile of shit, but the only thing he managed to prove is that he deserves to die.

He touched me without my permission. I said no, but he didn't listen. He is lustful toward me, and that's the only green light I need.

"Maybe we should go find somewhere more private to talk," I toss out with very minimal interest.

Still, he takes it as his open invitation to pull me closer and sniffs me like a fucking creep. I catch a whiff of stale beer on his breath, and he reminds me of my first kill, Gluttony.

"Yeah, I've got somewhere for us to go, pretty girl." He smiles, revealing a missing tooth, before grabbing my hand and pulling me down the street.

We stop in front of a door of what looks like an abandoned building with a steel rolled-down gate and graffiti covering it, and I make sure I keep my head down. My heart rate picks up as the man wiggles the door handle and pushes it open.

I start to wonder if maybe this was a bad idea and worry about whether or not there are other people inside the building. The last thing I need is to be reckless enough to end up in an entire homeless camp. I have a Taser and a knife, but that's not going to save me from an ambush. Stupid emotions.

"I don–" I start, but he interrupts.

"It's just us here. This is my secret place. I don't share." His eyes narrow at that last sentence.

Once inside, he pushes me up against the wall with a disgusting smile. His hands grope me through my hoodie as I reach into my bag to pull out the Taser. I waste no time bringing it up to his neck, hitting him with it twice while I pull my knife and gloves out.

He falls to his knees, screaming, and I kick him onto the ground with my foot. I hit him with the Taser again for good measure, and his body contorts to the side as his muscles seize up. He doesn't try to move, so I take the free moment to pull on my rubber gloves to keep the blood from getting onto my hands and then hover over him.

"Lust dies today," I say as I plunge the knife into his chest for the first time.

I puncture one of his lungs and let relief fill my veins. Feelings always overwhelm me with the first stab. As he begins to come back to reality from being tased so many times, he begs for me to stop. I bring the knife down a second time, hitting him on the opposite side of the chest. Then I stab him a third, fourth, and fifth with no defense.

My chest heaves as the adrenaline floods through me, and I pause for a second before plunging the knife into him the sixth time, watching as the life fades from his eyes. There's no reason for me to stab him again, but I do anyway because they all get seven.

Seven sins. Seven kills. Seven stabs.

I reach into my bag to pull out the rose and toss it on his chest. One final touch. It's a little smashed, but that doesn't matter. Now, I'll stop somewhere to place an anonymous call to the police about a noise complaint so they know to come here and investigate; otherwise, I doubt anyone will find his body any time soon if I don't.

After looking down at myself, I'm satisfied with how minimal the blood splatter was this time. There's a mirror in my purse that I use to check the exposed skin on my face for blood, and I only see one tiny spot that I wipe off with my hoodie.

Wearing black isn't just an aesthetic choice. It's also great for hiding blood. I pull my gloves off, placing them in the Ziplock bag that I brought inside my cross-body, and once they're safely secured in my purse, I take the hoodie off, turn it inside out, and slide it back on. I'll get rid of everything permanently like I always do when I get home.

One glance around the scene fills me with reassurance. I don't see any cameras inside, so I'm fairly sure I can leave without getting caught. I pull the hood back up and keep my head down as I quietly push open the door to make my way back to the Q.

The sooner I can get back to the hotel to get my shit, the better. Another job well done. Good riddance to this city until next year.

Chapter 8
Corbin - One year later

Today marks one year since I had a one-night stand with the mysterious cupid, who walked into my bagel shop, and I find myself questioning if she was even real at this point. Finding out she was connected to Drew was a sick twist of fate. Still, I was disappointed that by the time I put clothes on and made it down to the street, she was gone.

I suppose it's karma. I spent a good bit of my early twenties sneaking out of the beds of my random bar hookups, and the one time I actually felt a connection with someone, she pulled the same shit on me. She may not have snuck out, but she did run. So, same thing, but just a little different.

The one regret that stands out the most about that night is not finding out more about her before we slept together. Maybe it would have prevented the massive blow-up that things ended on.

The first month or so after she disappeared, I thought about trying to find her. I thought maybe it would be a romantic gesture or some shit to show up at her house with a bouquet of roses. I had her first name to go on and the very few details she told me about herself, which made it pretty easy to find her socials, but I couldn't pursue her.

Allowing myself to do that felt disrespectful after finding out she was connected to Drew. Even looking at her socials made me feel like a stalker. If she wanted me, that would be completely different, but she made it very clear she didn't want anything to do with me.

Her leaving affected me more than it should have. I've been pining after a woman I literally spent one night with. Trent made sure to point out how she must have a golden pussy because, according to him, it's impossible to believe there's any kind of woman out there who has that kind of power over a man. Fucking idiot.

Trent is still active in The Collection, unlike me, and has been complaining about how long it's taking for him to receive his assignment. Some would say I got out easy, even though I had to endure a near-death experience as well as the death of my wife. Maybe it's all about perspective, but it didn't exactly feel like getting off easy.

Rebecca Andrews died in a fatal car accident at the age of twenty-five. She was upset and swerved into oncoming traffic, only to be hit by a plow truck that killed her on impact. Rebecca was sweet; she didn't have to work, considering her family had the kind of generational wealth that we usually only hear about in movies.

It was old money, and as soon as her heart stopped, it became mine, or should I say The Collection's. Part of the initiation process required us to sign official documents stating anything we acquired during our time as active members would belong to them. I didn't care at the time because I was excited to be a part of something exclusive. I wasn't exactly the smartest person in my younger years.

The Collection doesn't care. They only care about wealth and how it can be used to their benefit because, at the end of the day, money is power. Whoever said money can't buy happiness clearly didn't have enough of it, at least according to them.

The thoughts have me shaking my head, annoyed. Everything I have was given to me under the pretense that if I followed their rules and kept silent, I would be able to keep it. The worst part is I did follow the rules, save the one slip-up that resulted in Rebecca's death.

They got my wife's inheritance, just like they wanted, and told me I fulfilled my duty to The Collection. I was free to choose whether or not I wanted to retire or take on a new assignment since I was still so young. That's what they call the women they expect us to win over, assignments.

I chose retirement, and they let me keep my apartment along with a hefty severance and an open threat that if I ever revealed The Collection in any way, it would be the last thing I did.

I was content with my life for years. Even though Rebecca died, I started the sandwich shop with my severance and poured all my time into it. Poppy left me questioning whether everything was worth it. Out of all the people in the world for me to fall into bed with, it had to be someone who was connected to one of my brothers.

Drew and I lost contact a long time ago, mostly because he went into hiding about two years before The Collection had him killed. He said he met someone and planned on leaving with her, then deleted all of his socials and any ties we had to him because he had no intention of following through with his assignment.

It pissed off whoever calls the shots from above, and even though it took them two years to track him down, ultimately they did. I don't know for sure who made the call to have him killed because there is so much secrecy surrounding who the higher-ups are, but they did.

We're all given a phone after initiation, and our orders appear on it as they're given. We're always provided with an address to a house where we can find a full paper file on our assignment, and then they only check in periodically as we are left to do our work. The only members most of us know are those who are inducted with us. Legacies would obviously know their parents too, but my parents died a long time ago.

My brothers. Four remain active members, while the fifth is cold and buried in the ground.

I understand why Drew was so taken by Poppy. She has this aura to her that you can't help being drawn to. The woman had me wanting to crawl around and worship her after one day. It's hard to imagine what I would have been willing to do if we spent longer together. None of that matters anyway. She left town, and I have to respect her wishes.

Part of me is surprised The Collection didn't kill Poppy for unknowingly disrupting the path of one of their members. They've been known to do much worse to the loved ones of members who are derailed just because they can. I've heard sometimes they make the members watch as the person they tried to flee for was killed in front of them. It's all rumors, but Poppy doesn't know how lucky she is to still be breathing.

I still think of her almost daily, and if she were to walk into my shop today, I think I would hear her out. I never believed in love at first sight, but I felt something rare for her, fuck, I still do.

From my office, I hear a loud disturbance in the shop. I've hired a few more people, so I don't have to work the counter myself now unless I want to, and I rarely want to. The yelling continues to grow louder, which annoys me. Kyle should be able to handle a simple irate customer. It's really not that difficult.

"Boss!" Kyle yells, and I let out a deep sigh.

"Yep, coming," I say as I close out of the tab on my laptop and slam it shut.

I pause at the doorway, giving myself a moment to get my shit together. My mood is already trashed, and trying to avoid snapping at the customer would be ideal, considering word of mouth is everything around here. Social media made this shop well known, and it would only take one viral video to take that away.

"How can I help y–" I stop mid-sentence.

There she is. The woman who's been stuck in my head for the past year, just standing in my fucking bagel shop like nothing happened. My eyes roam her body, taking in every inch of her. She's wearing damn near exactly what she was the first time she was here.

"You have got to be fucking kidding me," I let slip, and she raises a brow.

"I don't think that's an appropriate way to talk to your customers." A half grin appears on her face, but it pisses me off.

"I tried to tell her you were busy, but she insisted on speaking with the owner," Kyle says. "She threatened to stab me if I didn't call for you."

"Murder, really?" I turn my gaze toward her and lift my brow in question.

"I mean, it worked." She shrugs, and I grow increasingly irritated.

"Maybe we should take this to my office."

"Scandalous," she says, bringing her hand up to her mouth while I gesture with my arm for her to follow me. "Does everyone who causes a scene here get the same treatment?"

"Cupid. Go, now."

"Don't call me that. And did you forget you don't get to tell me what to do? You can talk to me right here." Her arms cross over her chest, and she stays firmly planted in place.

I hate that she's making me look weak in front of Kyle, but I must admit seeing her again has evoked the same submissive feeling it did the first time. My body craves her direction, and right about now, I would do just about anything she asked if it meant I got to have an actual conversation with her. I hate to admit it, but the last thing I want is for her to turn around and run again.

"Why are you here, Poppy?"

"I want a bagel. You still make them, right?"

"I could have made you a bagel, miss," Kyle says, but we ignore him.

"A bagel?" I question.

"Let's see if my memory will fail me or not. I'd like a jalapeno cheddar bagel with pastrami, egg, cheddar cheese, scallion cream cheese, and brown mustard. I believe you referred to it as "an orgasm in your mouth." Her eyes meet mine, and I step behind the counter to make her the sandwich just like I did a year ago when this all started.

Chapter 9
Poppy

"You lied to me," I say as he gets to work making the bagel.

His employee, Kyle, sneers before turning and walking into the back room, leaving Corbin and me to ourselves. For a brief moment, I considered making Kyle this year's kill for being an uptight asshole. That may not be good for Corbin's business, though.

I haven't been able to get him off my mind for the last 364 days, so here I am. I've had a lot of thoughts consuming me since spending time with Corbin, like whether or not Drew was actually connected to this so-called Collection. It took some time to muster up the courage, but eventually, I scoured our home for any sort of connection.

I was pretty close to calling it quits and chalking everything up to Corbin being a liar when I found a loose floorboard with a phone hidden inside. The phone was dead, with no way to turn it on, and when I looked further into the hidden spot, I found a letter. The letter went into detail, confirming everything. He explained that if I was finding it, then there was a good chance he was already dead. It touched on how The Collection operated and that I should keep this a secret because it could get me killed.

The note went on to say, he wanted me to move on because my happiness was his priority over everything, even if that meant I ended up with someone else. He ended the note with a starred message showing a phone number and told me if I was ever in trouble, I could call for help. Curiosity got the best of me, so I looked it up, only to find it belonged to Trent.

The Trent that was at the club the night Drew and I met and was also at the bar last year with Corbin. He changed a lot over the years, so I didn't recognize him at first, but he is the same person. Everything was all connected in some fucked up twist of fate. No fucking way would I ever call him.

For months, I read the letter over and over, taking in every detail and trying to figure out what it meant for me moving forward. Did I still feel obligated to uphold my promise of seven kills? Why didn't he tell me about The Collection sooner?

There must have been hints that I missed along the way. If I thought hard enough about our time together, I could probably pick some out, but I don't want to dissect our relationship. There would have been no way for me to ever guess he was hiding something that major from me.

A hand with a bagel reaches out, interrupting my thoughts.

"Are you going to ignore me?" I glare.

"The sandwich is on me. Now, if that's all, I have a lot of work to do."

"What, no catch like last year? You're just going to give this to me and walk away?"

"I don't know what you expect from me, Poppy. If you want to talk, we can, but I'm not doing it here. This is my business, and you knew that when you came in."

"Can we go back to your place?" I suggest, dropping the act. The truth is, I want to talk. The conversation has played on repeat in my mind for a year now, and I've pictured a million different ways that it would go. "We do need to talk."

"Do you think you can stay for the entire conversation this time?" he throws back. It's a low blow, but it's fair.

"I won't leave unless you want me to," I reassure him and watch as the expression on his face relaxes slightly. His jaw tics, like he wants to say something else, but he only nods before walking to the back.

He and Kyle return a few minutes later, and Kyle tosses me another dirty look. His scowl would scare me if I were a normal woman, but I'm a serial killer. I smirk to myself, thinking about how he doesn't even realize he should be afraid of me.

"Ready?" Corbin asks, and I nod as he leads us out of the shop.

He hails a cab, and the two of us sit in silence. There is so much more tension now that we're in a smaller space and it has me wondering if this was a mistake.

I glance down at the spot where my knee touches his leg, and the heat from the contact is all I can focus on. My mind is telling me to move, but I can't because I missed his touch.

Why does he affect me like this? If I were still friends with Lilly, she would ask me if he had a magic dick. That must be what it is. I was lulled into some sort of twilight zone where I can't stop thinking about a man all because he has a magic dick.

I chuckle to myself and see Corbin's head turn toward me in my peripherals. "Something funny?" he asks.

"I was having a debate in my mind about whether or not you have a magic dick," I blurt out in honesty.

His mouth drops open like he's going to say something, but it quickly snaps shut, and he shakes his head. When we pull up to his apartment building, I can't help the way my heart begins to race. A crippling anxiety begins to consume me, but I push that feeling away.

Suck it up, Poppy. This is why you went to his shop. You need your answers, and you need to know if how you felt toward him was real. I remind myself, even though part of me knows the things I felt, no... feel, for Corbin are definitely real.

How do I know that? Well, because I'm feeling them again now. It still doesn't make sense, and I don't particularly like it. Having feelings means losing control. Emotions only cause problems, and the last time I let go of control, someone I loved died.

After what feels like forever, we make it into his apartment, and I lean down to take off my boots before placing them on the same shelf I sat them on a year ago. I straighten myself only to see him standing just a few feet away, watching.

His chest heaves up and down, and his nostrils flare as his eyes stay trained on mine. I take a step toward him, closing the distance while imitating the same heavy breaths he seems to have. The air around us is electric, just begging for someone to break the tension, so I do.

"Kiss me," I plead. "Kiss me, now, before I lose every bit of courage and–"

I'm cut off when his mouth lands on mine, and my eyes fall closed. My body relaxes into him as his hands roam up and down my back, gently pulling at my hair. A soft moan leaves me, and his hand slides up to cup my face.

He deepens the kiss, like he's been starved for me, and the two of us move together before I'm pinned against the wall. His other hand slides down my waist, gripping me tightly before moving up to cup my breast through my sweater.

Fingers pinch my nipple, and my pelvis lifts into him. I can feel the hardened outline of his cock pushing into my stomach just begging to be touched. *Hmmmm begging sounds nice.*

I pull back, and he peers down, trying to catch his breath as I say, "I liked you better on your knees, bagel boy."

His eyes darken while he slowly sinks to his knees in front of me. He didn't even hesitate. I throw one of my arms over his shoulder while the other cups his cheek, letting him lean into it with closed eyes.

"You feel it, too?" It seems like an absurd question for me to ask, but for some reason, I can tell he understands.

"It doesn't make any sense," he admits, shaking his head.

"No, it doesn't, but I haven't been able to stop thinking about you—about us. We aren't even an us, but I can't get you out of my head. How is that possible?" My brows furrow as tears blur my vision.

"Sometimes things can't be explained, cupid, only felt. What I feel for you is different than anything I've ever felt in my life."

My eyes close for a brief moment while I reconcile my next moves. The first time I was here, I could say I was lonely and looking for someone for comfort, but being with Corbin this time is a choice.

It's my choice to move on from Drew and allow the possibility of someone else fulfilling the role that he was intended to. It's a choice to start living for my future instead of being consumed by my past. It's the exact choice Drew described he wanted me to make in the letter he left.

"Take the thoughts away. Remind me how good we are together," I say to Corbin with a smile, and he springs into action.

He stands from his kneeling position and lifts me in one fluid motion. My legs wrap around his waist, my arms around his neck as his mouth lands on mine again. We move steadily to his bedroom while we lose ourselves in one another. With the amount of desperation, you would think we were two lovers who just found one another after being forced apart for years.

He drops me down on the bed and reaches up to grip the waistband of both my leggings and panties, pulling them down and tossing them over his shoulder. Feeling his hands on my bare skin ignites a raging inferno, burning me from the inside out. Just one simple touch from him is all I need to be completely consumed again.

"I'm doing it my way this time," he asserts, and I don't tell him no because I want everything he has to give. "You have no idea how many times I've thought about doing this again, cupid." He pushes my legs apart, and I feel his breath meet my center.

Cupid. That stupid nickname. Who knows if he will still want to do this with me after he finds out I'm The Cupid Killer. I have to tell him the truth, even if he feels compelled to tell the police. I never planned to make it out of this alive anyway.

His tongue glides along my pussy and pulls me back to the moment. I bring my hands down to grip his hair, pleasantly surprised with the new length. It's grown about another inch and adds a new mischievous sex appeal to him.

His heated gaze lands on mine as he twirls his tongue inside me, making me rock my hips. I grip his hair harder, pulling him toward my clit as his tongue sweeps along my entrance. He groans but complies, latching onto my clit and making me see stars.

The pleasure builds faster than I could have ever imagined as he hums in approval while slipping a finger inside me and curling it in the perfect position. I whimper, letting him keep up the pace for another few moments before I can't take it anymore. I erupt, clenching around his finger while moaning his name. "Corbin."

When I start to come down, he pulls away long enough to walk over to the nightstand, grab a condom, strip free from his clothes, and slide the condom on. His eyes are dark and full of need when he makes his way back to me, possessed by lust.

I glance at the scars on his stomach, and I kick myself for not giving him the chance to tell me about them last year. Hands grip my ankles, and I'm pulled to the edge of the bed, making me giggle.

He throws my legs over his arms and slams into me unforgivingly, with no warning. Pleasure jolts my core, making my eyes roll back in my head, and I'm reminded of exactly how good sex with him is. He grins as his pace quickens, making my back arch off of the bed as his piercing rubs against my inner walls.

"So good," I breathe out, "you're so good for me."

That seems to encourage him a bit because he thrusts harder, determined to make up for any missed time we had.

"Fuck, keep doing that. Just like that," I whine, already feeling my body building again.

"Anything for you, cupid," he says while bringing a thumb to my clit and lightly pinching it between his fingers. My eyes shoot open as the combination of pain and pleasure sends me over the ledge.

"That's it. Come all over my cock," he growls, and I do exactly that with my pussy pulsing around him.

I clamp down and scream in pleasure as waves of what feels like electric shocks rush through me, and I come. He follows closely behind, shooting his release into the condom and grunting my name. "Poppy."

Chapter 10
Corbin

I pull out, and she scoots fully onto the bed without saying another word. Her eyes bounce around the room nervously, and I'm not really sure what to do now, which makes things a little awkward. We're apparently good at sex and not so good at the talking bits. Turning on my heels, I go to the bathroom to wash myself off and toss out the condom.

I'm supposed to be mad at her for what she did last year, but being around her makes it so hard.

When I return, she's already dressed and sitting at the edge of the bed while toying with her fingers in her lap. She glances over with a conflicted look, and I can't stop myself from being an asshole.

"Was that all you came here for?"

"You really think that?" Her eyes droop, and she seems hurt by the accusation, but what am I to believe?

"I'm sorry. I'm just worried you're going to take off again, and I won't see you for another year."

"I told you we needed to talk, and I came here to do that. I wasn't planning on..." she trails off and closes her eyes to take a deep breath.

I grab my clothes off the floor, deciding this conversation will probably go better if I'm not the only one naked, and then head toward the living room. "Come on. We can talk out here."

I sit in the chair, giving her the loveseat across the room, and wait for her to tell me whatever prompted her return visit. When her eyes meet mine, there is some sort of faint resolution in them, like she's reconciling something in her mind.

"When I met you last year, I planned on killing you."

"Yeah, that's not exactly the way to win someone over." I raise a brow.

"Can you just let me say what I need to say? It will be less confusing that way."

"Sure, cupid, have at it." I lean back in the chair and rest one of my ankles on my knee.

"Drew was killed on Valentine's Day. You said it was a hit by The Collection, but I didn't know anything about them. What I experienced was my fiancé being brutally murdered right in front of me by a man shouting about the Seven Deadly Sins."

"Fuck." I let my foot fall to the floor as I lean forward, placing my elbows on my knees.

"The guy stabbed him seven times, and when he was confident Drew was dead, he came after me. Luckily, someone intervened before he could kill me too, but it felt like he took everything from me that day. He even made sure to kill himself before the cops came so there would be no justice. Until I met you, the only thing I had to live for since that day was vengeance."

"What do you mean?"

"That nickname you call me. What if I told you there are other people who call me that, too?"

"Other people like who?" I say curiously. She has my full attention at this point.

"The cops. I'm The Cupid Killer. I've killed someone every year for the last six years, choosing one of them to represent each of the seven deadly sins. Seven sins, seven murders. I promised Drew I would make this city pay for taking his life."

That is not what I expected her to say. My thoughts swirl. There's no way in hell this woman is The Cupid Killer. That doesn't make sense at all. She doesn't look like a killer. I guess people don't usually look like they kill people, but there's no way this beautiful black-haired, brown-eyed goddess sitting in front of me is a serial killer? She has to be fucking with me, although she did hold a knife to my throat last year. And she did threaten to murder Kyle.

"Nice try," I dismiss her, but she persists.

"Corbin, I'm not kidding."

If she is really who she's claiming to be, she might be the most adorable serial killer out there. I chuckle to myself, deciding to keep that thought in my head because I highly doubt she would want to be called adorable right now.

"Okay, so you kill people. Why would you tell me that? Why confess now if you promised to kill seven? Aren't you worried I might call the cops and have you arrested before you can fulfill your promise?"

"You're not going to call the cops." She seems sure of herself, and I watch with annoyance as a smug grin crosses her face.

"You're sure of that?"

She pushes off the loveseat and crosses the room before slipping onto my lap, straddling me. Her fingers reach out to play with the collar of my shirt as she runs a finger along my jawline before tapping my chin.

"You won't call the cops because you like being a good boy for me." She leans in to whisper in my ear as my cock hardens under her. "Good boys don't call the cops, bagel boy. Good boys do as they're told and then beg for more."

I groan, her words going straight to my dick as she runs her nose along my neck. My hands grip her waist, holding her in place while I try to keep myself under control. With her sitting on me like this, all I can think about is her riding my cock until she screams my name.

There are too many things for us to talk about. We can't just fall back into the comfort of intimacy. We need to finish this conversation first. She's right about one thing. I would never call the cops on her because I don't give a fuck that she kills people. My moral compass isn't exactly in a place to judge others, and I kind of like that she's a little broken like me. Maybe our two broken halves will make us whole together.

"I'm not going to call the cops on you, Poppy."

She tries to slide off of me, but I hold her firmly in place. She leans in to press a chaste kiss to my lips, and a thought crosses my mind. She said lust was supposed to be easy before she ran off last year. Why didn't she kill me?

"Why didn't you kill me?"

"I couldn't. You're a good guy. There was no reason for me to kill you." She sighs, closing her eyes for a moment before she looks at me and places her palm against my cheek. "The only other time I've felt a pull this strong toward another person was with Drew. I couldn't kill you because I wanted you, fuck, I still want you, and it scares the shit out of me. That's why I ran off last year. I couldn't face the fact that I ended up captivated by someone I was supposed to kill. It made me feel weak."

"You're not weak, cupid."

"Aren't I?" She purses her lips. "It doesn't matter. Also, I was serious when I said you lied to me at your sandwich shop. You told me you weren't married, but I did my research, and you were."

This time, I let her slide off my lap. I knew it was only a matter of time before I had to tell her about Rebecca, but I didn't want her to judge me for it. It's not something I'm proud of.

"Her name was Rebecca," I start.

"I know what her name was, and I know that she died. I saw the news article talking about the car accident. What really happened?"

"The Collection happened." I crumple into the chair as my shoulders slouch over. "They wanted her money, so they made sure they got it."

"They killed her?" She raises a brow.

"I never loved Rebecca. I married her because she was assigned to me. It was my duty to The Collection to secure her fortune for their favor. Going against them is a death sentence, as you unfortunately had to learn the hard way when Drew tried to flee to be with you."

I pause, looking over at her tear-filled eyes, and resist the urge to comfort her. That can wait until everything is out on the table and she decides whether or not she wants to risk being with me.

"Rebecca started asking too many questions. It was my fault. She saw my phone and read through a strand of messages from the higher-ups because I fucked up. They were telling me I needed to secure an heir with her to ensure her fortune wouldn't escape their grasp from a technicality if I couldn't continue to pretend to love her. When she saw the messages, she lost her shit."

I run my hand through my hair, filled with nothing but shame. Rebecca's death has haunted me for years, and this is the first time I've talked about it with anyone. Even when Trent asked, I shut that shit down. It's bringing back harsh memories that cut fucking deep.

"I told her not to, but she used the phone and messaged them, saying I would never secure a child with her and that she was divorcing me. She told them nobody would get a penny of her family's fortune, so they retaliated."

"They killed her over money," Poppy breathes out, with disgust.

"We lived here together, and she tried to run out of the apartment, but I stopped her. I begged her to let me explain things and told her that if she was willing to keep up the ruse, I would find a way to keep us safe. As long as they thought they were going to get what they wanted, we would have been okay. Just because I wasn't in love with her doesn't mean I didn't care for her. I'm not a monster."

"That's a lot to ask of someone, Corbin. She thought you loved her; of course she would want to get away," Poppy tries to reassure me.

I reach over my head to pull my shirt off and gesture toward my scars. "These are from her. When I wouldn't let her leave, she grabbed a knife from the kitchen and stabbed me. She was in a full-blown panic, screaming about how I was a terrible person. When the first cut didn't take me down, she cut me again and again until she felt safe enough to flee. She didn't even realize I would have never hurt her."

Thinking back on everything, I realize it's kind of a full-circle moment. I had a knife pulled on me by two different women here. Apparently, I have a type, and it's women who are prone to stabbing.

"The scars are from her?" Her eyes widen.

I know she probably thought The Collection gave them to me, and in a way, they did. Poppy and I both carry scars because of them. The only difference is that mine are visible.

"She was scared, so she reacted. I don't blame her, but The Collection was ready to spring into action as soon they got the message on my phone. Someone was waiting for her outside the apartment. They grabbed her and staged her death to make it look like a car accident."

"If they took people from both of us, I wonder how many others are out there suffering too," she says, and I'm not sure I like the way her mind is processing this information.

"They painted a narrative that someone broke into the house to try and kill me, and Rebecca ran to get away. The cops claimed she was driving erratically, swerving into oncoming traffic. She was hit by a snowplow and killed on impact. I just didn't know it at the time because I was bleeding and being loaded into an ambulance so they could take me to the emergency room."

I run my finger along the bottom scar, letting the painful memories fill me for the first time in years. Rebecca lost her life, and the only thing I did was retire from The Collection, happy to be free of my duty to them. Poppy lost Drew, and she went on to kill people to get vengeance for him. This woman is so much stronger than she gives herself credit for. She's a better person than me, that's for damn sure.

Chapter 11
Poppy

I try to imagine how different today would have been if Corbin hadn't survived his stab wounds.

At the beginning of this quest for vengeance, I always planned on my last murder taking place in year seven. One for each of the deadly sins. Although, after having a taste of how it feels, I found myself wondering if I'd truly be able to stop.

Over the years, I considered everything and decided the only way for this to truly be over was if I became my seventh kill. I would get to be with Drew, and while it may not be exactly what he wanted for me, I highly doubt he would want me to spend the rest of my life in jail.

Corbin changed everything. He reminded me what it feels like to live again. I was dead on the inside for so long, but he managed to awaken my heart. It's finally beating toward the future, and I don't want to be my seventh kill.

I want to explore our connection because I'm almost positive he feels the same way. It's unfathomable considering how little time we've actually spent together, but when you know something is right, you just know. Why else would he even give me the time of day after I left the way I did last year?

Somehow, the broken parts of our souls intertwined with one another, upheaving our trauma and forcing us forward. We were both frozen in the past, but slowly, we're healing.

I definitely wasn't expecting him to be okay with me being a serial killer, so I turn toward him to talk about it a little more. "I'm not going to lie. I thought the whole 'I'm a serial killer' thing would be a bigger deal. You seem like you're okay with it," I say, testing the waters.

"Did you kill people who deserved it?"

"I did. They were all men who lived up to whatever sin I chose for the year. The first kill was a man trying to assault a woman."

"You sound more like a vigilante than anything else."

I laugh at that suggestion. "The police don't consider me a vigilante. I do appreciate the difference in outlooks, though."

"You said you have seven kills over seven years. Have you killed this year yet?" He asks a loaded question that I don't want to confess the answer to.

"I kill on Valentine's Day, and that's not until tomorrow." It's not a lie, although I'm leaving out some of the truth.

"Do you have someone chosen to kill tomorrow? It's not me, is it? I mean, now you know I'm not a good guy, even if that's what you thought before. I'm retired from a secret society and the reason my wife died. I lied to you about her."

"I'm not going to kill you, Corbin. If that were what I planned, I wouldn't have slept with you first."

"Just tell me, cupid. I can see you're struggling with something."

"The seventh kill was going to be me. I was going to confess to the murders with a letter and take my life the same way I did the rest of them."

"You're not doing that," he states plainly. He cares about me, and he doesn't want me to hurt myself. It's cute.

"I know. I changed my mind, but I don't know how I feel about that because that means my promise to Drew is unfulfilled."

"That doesn't have to be true. You can find someone else."

I could, but I don't know if I want to. I'm not angry at the city anymore. That anger has shifted to The Collection. They're the cause of all of this. So much unnecessary pain just to fill the pockets of men who most likely have tiny dicks.

The Collection didn't care about me because I didn't come from wealth. I wasn't even a significant enough person for them to eliminate after they killed Drew. That may be the part that stings the most. They weren't worried about me.

Something about that sparks a new vengeance deep within. My promise to Drew melds into something new that will have the men of that stupid society quaking in their penthouses. There's no limitation on how many years it will take or how many people will come to their untimely demise. Part of me did die today, and a new part was born in its place.

Drew's death awakened the killer in me, and this will see it blossom. The Collection didn't fear me before, but they will now. Everyone will fear my wrath because I'll be there to destroy what they built, brick by brick, no matter how long it takes.

"You look like you're up to something, cupid."

"Corbin, I have a question."

"Yes?"

"That spare room, is it empty? I need a place to stay."

"Don't take this the wrong way because I would love to have you around, but why would you stay in the city? I figured you would make your kill tomorrow and be on your way."

"Before I came here, I sold my house and pretty much everything I own because I planned on dying or turning myself in. I'm not going to kill someone tomorrow. Things have changed. It's going to be much bigger than that." An evil grin spreads across my face. "They're all going to die."

"Who?"

"Your Collection. I'm going to find out everything I can about them and destroy it all. I won't leave them out there to continue altering lives just so they can fill their pockets at everyone else's expense."

"Poppy, their influence runs deep. Do you really think you can take them down?"

"I think you underestimate my perseverance. When someone tells me I can't do something, my only response is to say, watch me." I nod my head to myself, knowing I will devote my entire life's purpose going forward to making this a reality if I have to. I will end them or die trying. "My final kill is going to be The Collection."

"I'll help you then. We won't stop until we take them down," he says in a stance of solidarity. "You'll be my own little bloody valentine, cupid."

"I like the sound of that." I giggle, my eyes filling with lust as my gaze lands on his. "Corbin," I say, curling a finger in his direction. "Come here."

He stands and goes to take a step toward me, but I hold out my hand and shake my head.

"Crawl to me and worship me," I say, scooting to the edge of the loveseat.

He pauses for a moment, eyes darkening before he falls to his hands and knees. He inches forward, little by little, doing exactly what I asked before he finally stops in front of me and leans back on his heels. His hands glide up my legs from my ankles to my knees before he gently pushes them apart and positions himself between them.

"You're wearing too much clothing," he teases, pressing a kiss to my thigh.

I groan, knowing he's right, as I hook my thumbs into my leggings and underwear before sliding them off. He aids me in the process, wasting no time making himself at home between my legs again.

"My favorite place to be." He grins before leaning in and sweeping his tongue along my pussy.

I will never get enough of this man or how amazing he is at giving me pleasure. My enjoyment means more than his own, and that thought has me pushing back on his shoulders. He deserves a reward.

"Stop," I command, leaving him confused, but he listens. "Take your pants off and come here." I pat on the vacant seat next to me.

Once he does, I stand and get him repositioned so that he's lying on the loveseat with his legs hanging over one end and his head folded up a little on the other.

"I thought a good boy like you deserved a nice little treat."

"Are you going to sit on my face, cupid?"

"Maybe."

"Fuck," he groans. "Get that pussy over here. Please don't make me wait."

"I love it when you beg." I lean in to kiss him, tasting myself on his lips.

When I pull back, I slide one leg over his waist, facing the opposite direction, and slowly scoot my ass backward until my pussy hovers over his face. He grips my hips and pulls me down, not hesitating to dive right in.

"Yes," I moan as I lean forward and grip his hardened cock.

His tongue swipes up and down, lapping me up as one of his fingers finds its way to my clit. I lean forward and slide my tongue up the length of his shaft, making him shudder beneath me.

The power I feel as I swirl my tongue around his tip and then flick it against his piercing is beyond words. His hips buck forward, wanting more, as he pulls me up from his face to speak.

"You're a fucking goddess, cupid. Please suck my cock. Give me that mouth, baby."

When he pulls my pussy back down to his face, his fingers find my clit again. He grins against me, rubbing quickly as my focus falls back on his hard length and my mouth closes around his tip.

I glide my mouth down his cock, slowly taking every bit of him before I begin bobbing up and down. The piercing feels weird when it hits the back of my throat, but I get used to it as I find my pace.

He moans against me when I bring a hand up to place it at his base, moving it up and down in tune with my mouth. It's a sloppy mess, but I don't think either of us cares. My tongue swirls around his cock over and over while he rubs my clit.

I whimper around his cock. The combined sensations of his touch have my body buzzing, so I suck him harder and faster. I need him to come for me before I explode.

His hips push up, making me gag, but I don't stop. We work together, both of us doing everything we can to bring one another to bliss. My pussy spasms against his tongue, and I feel his dick twitch in my mouth.

At this point, it's a game to see who will find their release first, and he's determined to make sure it's me. He picks up his pace, licking faster, and I lose. My body erupts in pleasure, and I scream around his cock while the tingles ripple through me. Just a few seconds later, he pulls his face from my center and says, "I'm going to come in that pretty mouth if you don't stop, cupid."

I keep up my pace, hoping he does exactly that, but he slaps my ass, making me jump. I lift my mouth off of him and scowl over my shoulder. "Why would you do that?"

"When I come, I want to feel your pussy gripping my cock. Let me grab a condom and fuck you right, please."

"Since you said please, I'll let it slide. You don't need a condom, though." I grin, not giving him a chance to ask if I'm sure before I slide my body forward, grabbing his shins and lowering myself onto his cock.

Feeling him bare is so much better than I could have ever imagined. I have to pause for a moment as I look over my shoulder again. He's up on his elbows this time, watching me intently.

"Lay back and let me use you, bagel boy."

"You don't have to tell me twice, cupid," he says as his back meets the loveseat again, and his hands find my hips.

"Good boy." I smirk before turning my head and beginning to bounce up and down on him. One of his hands falls from my waist to the side of my ass as I grind down.

"You feel so good," he praises, and it pushes me to move faster.

His hips begin thrusting up from under me, matching my pace and building the heat. I need more stimulation, so I bring a finger down to my clit and rub it while continuing to use him. Hands grip my hips tighter, and he grunts while thrusting up into me faster.

"Yes, baby. That's it. Make yourself come with my cock," he groans.

"Look at you, so needy. Let me hear all those pretty little sounds you make," I breathe out, using each one of them as fuel.

"Fuck, I'm going to bust," he says, making me that much more determined.

"Do it. Come for me like the desperate little bagel boy I know you are."

He groans again, and I rub myself faster while the roaring fire begins to blaze inside me. I slide up and down, once, twice, three more times before he curses, and I feel him jerking beneath me. My pussy clamps down, and I come with him while tipping my head back, screaming his name, "Corbin!"

My body slumps forward, and we take a few minutes to catch our breath before I slide off of him and fall to the floor. His release begins to drip out of me, and before I know what's happening, I'm being swept up and tossed over a shoulder.

"What are you doing!" I giggle.

"I'm taking you to bed so I can devour you for the rest of the day."

"It's barely one o'clock! We have to eat!" I protest when I feel a rumble in my stomach as he tosses me down.

"Oh, I'll eat," he tries, making me laugh as I slap him away.

"You're ridiculous. I need some sustenance first."

"I believe I made you a bagel before we came here," he counters.

"Yeah, about that. I didn't have time to eat it. It's still in my purse."

He brings his hand to his mouth, covering up a horrified look on his face. "You being a serial killer, I can excuse, but wasting a perfectly good bagel is criminal!"

"What can I say? I may be certifiably insane. You better watch yourself, considering you agreed to let me live with you." I sit up and cross my arms over my chest.

"Having you close just means you can't get away from me, pretty girl. I'm just protecting my assets."

"Oh, yours?" I raise a brow.

"If you want to be." He shrugs.

"I definitely want that," I say, making him smile as I slip away to go to the bathroom real quick.

When I come back out, he's lying on the bed, patting the spot next to him. Without hesitating, I crawl up and lay down, letting him pull me into the safety of his hold.

If you had asked me a year ago what my future would look like, it certainly wouldn't be this. Things are so different now. Corbin and I may not know everything about one another, but he feels like home.

He squeezes me tighter as if he's thinking the exact same thing, and I pull back a little bit to peer into his eyes, which are full of nothing but vulnerability. "It's you and me, right?"

"You and me, cupid. We're in this together," he reassures me as he leans in to press a kiss to my forehead.

I don't know what taking down The Collection will look like, but I know that with him by my side, they will feel my wrath. I've never felt more sure about anything in my life.

Epilogue
Poppy - 8 months later

"Are you sure this is a good idea? We should just go to the warehouse alone and check things out." I tilt my head in Corbin's direction for some reassurance because we've been driving for what feels like forever.

"No, we need help, and my initiation brothers are just as invested in taking down The Collection as we are."

"I told you I'd figure out how to handle them." I gruff in annoyance. The idea of trusting other people to assist with something so important makes me uneasy. "Do you really trust them?"

"I do. Not to mention, it's taking too long. We've been trying to get a solid lead with no luck for months. The only reason we got this one is because of Raiden. I want to be free of their hold so we can start our lives together. Don't you want that?"

I take a breath, knowing he's right. We've been inseparable since I showed up at his sandwich shop for the second time eight months ago. We got a new place, and things have been good. The only thing keeping our lives from perfection is this incessant need to destroy The Collection.

I want to be able to relax, settle down, maybe start a family, but I can't allow my mind to even think about that until I make them pay. They can't be allowed to continue ruining people's lives.

Finally, our destination comes into view, and we park next to the porch. It looks like a normal house. There's nothing that really screams "we're hosting a meeting about uncovering a secret society."

Corbin turns to look at me, bringing his hand up to cup my face, and I lean into it. "We're close. I can feel it. Let's do this so we can start our forever."

I smile as he leans in to press my lips to his, and I let all of my doubts slip away. We deepen the kiss, getting lost in one another before I pull back to catch my breath.

"I love you, cupid."

"I love you too, bagel boy. Let's get this over with. I'm dying to get back home so I can try out that new ball gag."

"If you're using it on yourself, then yes, but I already told you I'm not putting that thing in my mouth."

"I'll wear you down. You know you can't resist being a good boy for me." His nostrils flare, and I smile, knowing he can't deny it.

We walk hand in hand inside the house without bothering to knock or ring the doorbell, which I find a bit odd. Once inside, Corbin leads me to a living room with four people whose eyes all land on us at the same time.

"Poppy, these are my brothers," he says before pointing at each one and rattling off names.

Raiden, the brown-haired guy who oozes your typical alpha energy.

Casper, who apparently goes by Ghost and has the coolest neck tattoo I've ever seen.

Devlin, the blonde who seems a bit shifty.

I'm not introduced to the female who is sandwiched between Raiden and Ghost. They both have a hand on each one of her thighs, which I find interesting. Lucky girl gets two men to play with.

"Corbin." Raiden smirks. "How's retirement treating you?"

"Nice to see you too, asshole," Corbin says, making the other two guys laugh as he escorts me to a small vacant couch on the other side of the room.

As we pass the female, she holds out her hand, prompting me to shake it. "Hi, I'm Faylon."

"Poppy," I say with a smile before going to sit on the couch.

I glance around and notice there's someone missing. Trent. Maybe he's running late. Corbin must have the same thought because he vocalizes it almost immediately.

"Where's Trent?"

"Who the fuck knows. The weasel probably got sidetracked in someone's vagina." Raiden shrugs.

Corbin pulls out his phone to send a quick text while eyeing the time. We're already fifteen minutes behind schedule and can't wait for him if we want to make it to the warehouse on time to catch the meetup.

"We'll start without him," I say, taking point in the meeting. I'm not sure what everyone's vibe is, but I want to make it known from the start that I won't be a bystander.

Raiden nods. "The information I overheard from my father was that they're meeting at a warehouse ten minutes away from here. I don't think there will be security with them since the meeting is supposed to be a secret, but there's no way to know for sure."

"I doubt they will bring security. That would draw attention. You know they're all about being as discreet as possible," Devlin says, which makes sense.

"Did you bring the guns I asked you to?" Corbin asks Ghost, and he nods, not bothering to verbalize his response.

"There's no reason to make this complicated. We all get guns, and we go in at the same time. If they put up a fight, we shoot them," I state.

"Violent little thing." Raiden raises his brow.

"You have no idea," Corbin chuckles before turning to me. "Calm down, my little bloody valentine. We need them alive."

As bloodthirsty as I am, he's right, but I still roll my eyes. "Fine. I won't kill all of them yet. But once we have what we need, can I kill them?"

Corbin smiles and nods, but when I turn to look at the others, I find them wide-eyed and speechless. I don't know why it's so hard for people to believe women are capable of murder, too.

"Faylon will be staying in the car once we get there," Raiden says, and I see her elbow him in the ribcage. "I'm not waiting in the car. I'm going in with a gun, just like everyone else."

"Do you even know how to use a gun?" he asks her.

"Want to find out?" she challenges, and he holds his hands up in defeat while shaking his head.

"Your funeral," Raiden concedes.

Ghost leans in to whisper something in her ear, and she laughs before leaning into him. Ghost and Raiden are like night and day, but it's obvious she cares for both of them. The different effects she has on each of them is cute. I can practically feel the tension between her and Raiden from here.

We spend the next 15 minutes going over every possible detail of how our plan will work, ironing out all the factors to prevent anything from going wrong. The grandfather clock in the corner of the room chimes, telling us it's time to leave. There are only thirty minutes until the scheduled meetup, and it's a ten-minute drive. We're not missing this.

One by one, we filter into our vehicles and drive to the warehouse. This town reminds me a lot of where I grew up. I wonder if Corbin will want to move to a place like this.

The car slows, and I know the time has come. We'll have our first glimpse at The Collection's higher-ups. Once we all gather in front of the door, I turn the handle slowly as the men stand beside me with their guns outstretched. We all filter in and are confused when we find the room empty, save the person secured to a chair in the middle with a bag over their head.

I can't help but let curiosity get the best of me, so Corbin and I walk over to the subdued person, and I rip off the bag. Shock courses through us as we glance down to find the last person we expect to see, Trent. That would explain why he didn't meet us at the house earlier.

Trent looks around the room with a sinister smile. "You don't even know the mess you've gotten yourselves into. They're coming for all of you now."

Corbin punches him in the face. "You slimy little fucker. You tipped them off. I thought we were friends."

"I was keeping an eye on you. You're the reason I haven't been given an assignment yet. They've been waiting for you to fuck up. You just had to bring the rest of our brothers down with you, though, didn't you?"

"I know what this is. Daddy told you to get in line so you wouldn't be a disappointment. You're always trying to find ways compensate for your little dick," Raiden tosses out. He moves to stand next to Corbin and me as he glares down at Trent. "How did that all work out for you? Clearly, they don't give a fuck about your life either."

Trent opens his mouth, but I decide he's taunted everyone in this room enough. The only way to get him talking about something that actually matters is by force. I've been itching to stab someone, so it's time to let my rage shine bright.

I whip out my knife and plunge it into his arm, smiling as he lets out an agonizing scream.

"Did she just..." Ghost says from the corner, surprising me. I honestly forgot he was even here.

"She did," Delvin reassures him.

The fact that men are amused so easily when a woman chooses violence is entertaining.

"I need you to teach me how to do that without hitting something important," Faylon says in astonishment.

"No. We don't need you running around with knives." Raiden shuts down her suggestion quickly.

I ignore him and smile at her while pulling the knife from Trent's arm. He's screaming something about how he's never going to tell us anything. Blah, blah, blah. We shall see. "Want to try? You can take the next stab."

She comes over in a rush, and I pass the knife along, pointing at where she should stab him. She plunges the blade into the meaty part of his thigh but struggles a bit to pull it out.

"You fucking bitch! I'll make sure they kill all of you," Trent calls out.

"That was pretty good. We should get lunch sometime, and I'll give you more pointers," I toss out to Faylon, and she nods enthusiastically.

"Sounds good to me," she says, making me smile. It might be nice to have another female friend in my life again.

"The last thing she needs is to learn how to stab men," Raiden mutters. "You're a bad influence."

Trent lets out a manic laugh that pushes me over the edge. He's treating this like it's just some minor inconvenience that he's going to walk away from, but that couldn't be any further from the truth.

"I suggest you start talking. Corbin and I have plans, and I'll be damned if some little shit like you is going to keep us from them," I state firmly.

Everyone has a weakness. You just have to know enough about them to find out what it is. Trent is about as transparent as they come. This may not be who we were expecting to find here, but I'm willing to bet if he's tied to the chair like this, he has some kind of knowledge that could be useful.

"Do you think he'll still be able to get laid if he's blind? Which eye should I gouge out first?" I press the tip of my knife into the corner of his eye, making him freeze.

He still doesn't say anything, so I push it in a little further. The edge pierces the skin next to his eye, and a small streak of blood begins to drip down. Trent is about as conceited as they come, so I push harder. I can almost guarantee threatening to disfigure his precious face will do the trick in three... two... one...

"Stop! I'll talk."

"Good boy." I smile with my eyes meeting Corbin's. He looks annoyed that I called Trent a good boy, but I'll be sure to make it up to him later. "Now, tell us everything you know about The Collection's higher-ups, and then I'll decide whether or not you've earned the right to keep breathing."

Coming soon...

Their Assignment

If you'd like to know more about how The Collection is taken down, be sure to check out Their Assignment, available now for preorder.

This story will follow Faylon, Ghost, and Raiden, featuring Poppy, and Corbin as side characters!

An official release date will be announced at a later time.

Acknowledgements

To all the readers who continue to make my dream a reality, thank you for taking a chance on me and my silly little stories.

Hubby, thank you for entertaining my need to hyper fixate and for being so understanding when I locked myself away for a solid two weeks to power through this. I love you!

Sarah, Jess, and Mickie, thank you ladies for being the best alpha team out there.

Haley, Jordon, Amanda, and Cass, my beta babes, you're all amazing! The fact that you all dropped everything and got this done means the entire world to me.

A special thank you to Rosie and Veronica for reading through and giving feedback on the NYC bits!

Taylor, you are the best editor a girl could ask for, as always, thank you!

To my author besties, Ivy and Maree, thank you ladies for giving me a space to always feel supported.

One final shout out goes to Sleep Token and their song Levitate. It was my go-to song to play before writing every day.

About the author

K.M. Baker is a Dark Romance author who lives in a small town in Pennsylvania with her husband. She has three dogs, two German Shepherds and a Bichon Frise, who are like children to her.

Writing has always been a dream, but she never had the courage to do it until recently.

Most of her free time is spent reading all the spicy books she can get her hands on (the dirtier, the better). Outside of reading, she enjoys gardening, crafting, and taking her 1972 Sprint Mustang to car shows. Coffee, red wine, and blankets are some of her favorite things to indulge in. She is passionate about traveling and hopes to one day move and live outside the US.

Stalk Me:

Tik Tok: @K.M.Bakerauthor

Instagram: @K.M.Bakerauthor

Facebook: K.M. Baker's Bookworms

Email: KMBakerauthor@gmail.com

Books by K.M. Baker

The Darkness Duet:
Evading Darkness
Darkness Falls

The Renegade Series:
Bloody Seven – A prequel novella
Their Assignment – Coming soon

Standalones:
The Afterthought
Endless